Bryant

PRINCE OF TIGERS BOOK 1

KATHI S. BARTON

This is a work of fiction. Names, characters, places, and incidents are products of the author's imagination or are used fictitiously and are not to be construed as real. Any resemblance to actual events, locations, organizations, or persons, living or dead, is entirely coincidental.

World Castle Publishing, LLC
Pensacola, Florida
Copyright © Kathi S. Barton 2019
Paperback ISBN: 9781949812923
eBook ISBN: 9781949812930
First Edition World Castle Publishing, LLC, April 22, 2019
http://www.worldcastlepublishing.com
Cover: Karen Fuller
Editor: Maxine Bringenberg

Chapter 1

Buck enjoyed hot wings, the hotter the better. But even he had to admit defeat when it came to eating wings with his oldest. Bryant would get them as hot as he could, then add more heat to them. Buck often wondered if the boy could taste a dammed thing after he ate a plate of them suckers.

Today he was eating alone. He didn't get that opportunity much, not since his Sara had been killed all those years ago. But it was her birthday, and while he knew that his boys were remembering her today, he had his own way of thinking about his little mate.

When the plate was set in front of him, he looked up at the waitress. Deb had been working here since she was a teenager. He wondered if they'd built the place around her. When she winked at him, he smiled back. Everyone was aware of his way of doing things.

The first one always made him tear up — the heat, not his heart, he told himself. But as he was picking up the second one to eat, Bryant came into the diner. Whatever had happened, it had Buck reaching for his pistol that he was never without.

"It's all right. I just wanted to come tell you before you left here and found out the hard way." Bryant then told him how sorry he was for coming here, today of all days. "Pops, there's been a fire at the Wilson home. The mister is dead, and his wife, she's on her way to the bigger hospital for treatment. It doesn't look good for her either."

The Wilsons had the farm right next to theirs. The Wilsons had bought up a lot of land when they first arrived in this area, putting themselves and their kids in a powerful terrible place. The money had been plentiful when the Wilsons arrived. But planting things that the earth didn't have the energy to grow made for bad years of bringing crops in. That's why Buck's family only had a dozen acres, as well as cattle.

"The kids home?" Bryant shook his head, still not sitting down with him. "No, they'd not be there for any reason, would they? What else, boy? You know I don't care for things being given out in little bits and pieces."

"Samson and I were wondering if we should take in their crops for them. The mister, he's not there anymore, and you know as well as I do that the kids wouldn't come back to help if their very lives depended on it. Not that I blame them any, but the missus, she might pull through, and the money might make the difference in her having medicine or not." Buck stood up, his meal ruined now. Not by his son, no; the news was what had soured his taste. "I'm assuming that's a yes."

"Gather up the boys, Bryant, and we'll get a start on it for sure." Buck went to pay his bill, and Deb told him that there was no charge. "I have to keep you in business, Deb. If I don't, where will I get to come for breakfast every day?"

"Here, just like you do every day, you old coot. I heard

6

what you're doing, and I've called my sons. They're going to meet you there to help out. I'll be bringing by some food about dinner time, and a cooler of drinks too." She shoved him out the door. "I have work to do, Buck. Now get on out of here so I can get to it."

By the time he'd gotten on his tractor and made his way to the next farm, there were about fifty men and women out there, all of them ready to work. With the extra hands and the other two tractors, he was sure they could get a lot of the fields picked and plucked in no time.

Buck worked with his boys. Men really, all of them as old as sin. It was the way of their kind, the first of their species. Immortality had been given to them when he and his wife had been created to give the earth some of their kind. A lot of their magic.

Sara and he had had six children, all of them from one litter. They'd been cats then, black tigers that had come to this earth with no ill will in their hearts. It was a good thing as well as a bad thing for them to be so trusting.

The day after his cubs had been born, the lady of the earth, Aurora, had come to see them. She thought them blessed to have so many sons at their only birthing. That was the downside, he thought — only one birthing to be bestowed to them. It was, she told them, to not overpopulate the world with such a special creature. Before the lady had shown up, they were going to call the boys by number of birth. And they did so until they were a little older and could pick out their own names.

"I shall wish for you to roam the earth as men as well as tigers, giving your magic to as many of those as you touch with kindness. I know by creating you that you are already kind and good hearted, but it is my wish that you spread it to all the humans as well. I fear that they're going to be much worse as the years go by."

And she'd been right about that. Not that everyone they encountered was bad—no, there were a great many good people too. But the trouble was, he feared that they were slowly being outnumbered by the bad people in this world.

It was nearing ten when they finished up the last of the fields. Harley, his son, asked why they'd planted pumpkins. Buck didn't know, but he figured that they'd sell them in their roadside stand until they heard otherwise. Every little bit would help, he supposed.

Going home, he dusted the earth off his clothing and stripped down. Buck didn't look his age, he thought with a laugh. He could very well pass as one of his sons, and had on occasion. Shifting into his cat, he hit the ground running. He wasn't the least bit surprised to find Kylan out there running as well.

Are you all right, Kylan? He said that he was, just tired. *Yeah, so am I. But we did a good turn for those people. And that is what we were put here for.*

Is that all we were put here for, Pops? He asked him what he meant. *I'm lonely. I need more in my life than just farming and raising cattle. I have a degree — I'd like to branch out and start using it. It might, I hope anyway, bring in more money than just selling off cattle to the local farmers.*

All of them had gone to college. It hadn't been one of the ivy leagues—they couldn't swing that. But each of them had gone to the local college and had a nice degree to show for it. Kylan had a degree in advertising, and he could come up with ideas for things that would spin your head, as Sara used to say.

Then I'd say go for it. I'm getting a little tired of raising cattle myself. Not much in the way of money in it, not the way we're going. Kylan said he'd been talking to Marcus, and they wanted to open an advertising business together. *Well, with Marcus doing the art work, you'd sure be good at it, son. Both of you would be. And I know that Harley has a degree in business management. Perhaps that would be the ticket. Not all of you working in the same place. You know as well as I do that is just a fight waiting to happen.*

Kylan laughed. *Yes, I've noticed that as we've gotten older, the arguing becomes more dangerous.* They fought like men who hated each other. But as soon as someone drew blood, the fight was over and they were taking care of the injured one.

Kylan left him after their talk. He was going to go and get things started, Buck knew that. Making his way to the little cemetery that his wife was buried in, Buck laid down on the ground next to her and told her about his day, just as he did every night when he could.

Those boys, they're going to leave me soon, Sara. I don't know what I'm going to do in that house without them arguing all the time and picking at me. He smiled to himself. *They sure have grown into men of worth, my darling. I think we did a good job, not even knowing what we were about back then.*

He told her about the Wilsons and how they'd brought in their crops. They were going to try and get ahold of one of their children, to see what they wanted to do with it all. Buck had a feeling he knew what they were going to tell them—just to burn it all.

Pops, I hate to bother you, but I just heard that the missus, Mrs. Wilson, has passed on. She was pretty well burned all over her body, they said. And the fire marshal, he's saying that it looks like arson.

9

As soon as it cools down enough, they'll have a better idea. Buck thanked Fisher. *Also, I wanted to tell you that I'm very proud to be your son. I should be saying that more often. All of us should. What we did tonight, even though Bryant was the one that thought of it, you didn't hesitate for a moment to step in with us. I love you, Pops.*

For the next ten minutes or so, Buck laid there sobbing about what his son had said to him. It didn't hurt him, but his heart did burn with love for his sons. Telling his wife about the death and what his son had said, he stood up and made his way back to the house.

All the lights were on in the place, but he knew as surely as he was walking home that someone was in each of the rooms. They all knew the meaning of a nickel, and leaving the lights on when you left a room was a big deal.

There wasn't any need for him to get dinner started. True to her word, Deb had not only brought them out food, but it was the kind they could carry along with them as they worked. And there was plenty of her sweet tea and water. While normally Buck wouldn't care for the sweet stuff, it was mighty nice on a hot evening to have something that gave you a bit of pep.

Just as he was ready to go to bed, he glanced at his desk. It had been put up here because it was quieter in their room without the boys running around. Then when they'd gotten older, it had just been too much trouble to mess with.

Buck had gotten a card from one of the Wilson boys when his Sara had been killed. Looking for it now, he found it among some of the other things that he'd been meaning to take care of. It had been a few years, coming up on ten, since she'd passed, but Buck never threw anything away.

There was a return address on it, and Buck laid it right on

10

top of his pants he was wearing tomorrow so he'd remember to do that first thing. He didn't know if anyone in town would know how to contact the family, so he was going to do it. If they already knew, then that would be fine too. He could pass along his condolences and tell them about the product they'd pulled in for them.

Closing his eyes, he thanked the mother of the earth for his day and wished his wife a happy birthday. Rolling to her side of the bed, he spooned her pillow. It was as close to her as he could get nowadays.

~*~

Randy tried to remember Mr. Prince. He knew that it had been a while. He'd left home when he'd turned eighteen and had never looked back. Now he was successful, married, and had two children. And, his parents were both now dead.

"The fire was a big one, as you can imagine. They rushed your momma to the hospital by life flight, but she just couldn't make it. I'm truly sorry, Randy. We did help them out a bit by bringing in the crops that were still out. My sons, they're selling what we can at the stand we have out every year. We're keeping the money for you to use for —"

"Mr. Prince, while I do appreciate you doing everything you could for them, my sisters, my brother, and I, we don't want anything to do with them. I'm sorry that sounds so harsh, but we cut complete ties with them long ago." Randy sat down at the table. He felt like a shit hole for saying this aloud. "I'll pay for the funeral and whatever other expenses that they might have, but there isn't anything that would make me want to go back there again. I'm sorry."

"I know you kids had it bad, I do know that. I wanted to... well, Randy, you don't know how hard it was for my missus and me not to step in sometimes. Even with all the distance between the houses, we still heard it."

Randy thanked him. He wished he'd known that. He might have run to them when it was really bad. Which wasn't saying much—it had always been bad.

"Well, you tell me what you want done here and I'll help you out with it. I never cared for your parents, I'll tell you that. But we do like the land and what it represents to people."

"Yes, I'm sure that there are few people that cared all that much for my parents, Mr. Prince." Randy looked at the calendar on his desk. There was barely a minute to call his own. "I'll call my sisters and brother. See what it is they want to do. I'm sure that none of us will be making the trip for the funeral. So if you could see your way to getting that taken care of, I'll pay you back. Nothing big, just something quick and done."

"I'll get on that first thing. I'll let you know about when it is. I'll just have them a gravesite and bury them both at the same time. It might help you to know, if there was any insurance, that your father died first. Mrs. Wilson died last night." Randy thanked him. The man had always had the right amount of information to give someone without overwhelming you. "You let me know what you all decide. We're going to be working on selling off the crops and such. If it's enough, you might not be out of pocket anything."

After getting off the phone with the elderly man, Randy thought about what he'd said. The Prince family would have taken them in, he knew that now. It was too late, but they would have been there for them. Randy thought that had any of them known that, they would have been more well-adjusted adults and not afraid of every little sound—fearful of someone coming after them with a hot poker, or even a gun.

Randy called his sister Meggie first, and she reacted just the way he'd thought she would — by doing the happy dance, she told him, right there in her kitchen. He asked her if she wanted to go with him to settle their estate.

"Estate? You really think they were able to save any money after we left? We were always told what a terrible burden we were to them. I'm betting that they had no life insurance, no homeowners, nor anything on that property." She laughed bitterly. "No, I don't want to go unless I have to. And even then, I don't want to go. No, Randy, I'm over them. My life is finally on an even keel, and we both know how long that took me. Not to mention what it cost me."

"I know, honey. And I'm so sorry." Meggie's husband had divorced her and taken the little girl that they had. But not long after the divorce had been finalized, her ex and the little girl were killed in a plane crash. It had taken her years to get over that. "I'll take care of everything. Mr. Prince said he'd make the arrangements for us."

"He always was a very generous and nice man. The entire family was. I so wanted a family like that one, didn't you, Randy?" He told her that he had, and also what Mr. Prince had told her. "They didn't have squat, but they would have given us all they had if we needed it. Tell him that I said thanks."

"I will."

Now he had to call Harper, but he thought that he'd call Tyler first. Harper only lived down the street from his family after moving into a small condo about two years ago. It was both a pleasure and a nightmare to have her so close. Harper

13

didn't suffer fools lightly, nor did she have a filter between her brain and her mouth. Calling Tyler was much easier.

"Mom and Pops have both died," he started off. Tyler, like Meggie, laughed. Then Randy told him about the fire and how things were being done. "Mr. Prince, do you remember his family? He's taking care of the arrangements for us. And I'm going to take care of anything else that might have to be done. After the funeral. I was wondering if you wanted to go with me."

"No, and fuck no, I do not want to go." Tyler, a quieter version of Harper, then laughed. "No, if you want some company, I'll go with you, so long as you're one hundred percent sure that they're both gone. I don't have shit to say to them."

"Neither do I. Meggie isn't going. I called her first." Tyler made fun of him for waiting to call Harper last. "You would too if you had to make this call."

"Yes, you're more than likely right about that. She's a tad touchy about them." And she had every reason to be too. Harper, even being the youngest of them all, had endured the most from their parents. To this day she still — "I'm sorry, what did you say?"

"I said that I bet Harper will want to go for the simple reason that she wants to piss on their graves. Not to mention, I'm betting that before the end of the first day there, she has a certified letter stating that they're not only dead, but buried as well." Randy didn't think his brother was far off the mark. "Let me know what she's going to be doing, Randy. For now, I'll make sure that my calendar is clear for the next week. I know you'll have to take your computer, but we'll be there and back in no time."

"All right."

He put the phone in the cradle, thinking again that he was more than likely the only person in the world with a household phone still. It was for business and the fax machine. As he pressed the buttons for Harper's home, he wondered if she was in a more reasonable mood than she had been earlier today. Harper answered the phone like she and he had spoken not two seconds ago.

"Did you know that there are over nine hundred thousand different kinds of bugs in the world? Which accounts for over eighty percent of the world population." He told her that he'd not known that. "I'm sorry about earlier today. I tend to get my underwear all twisted up when I drive, you know."

"I do know, and cannot believe that you've not been arrested for it." She told him that she was cute. "You're not cute, Harper, you're gorgeous. Everyone but you knows that. Now, the reason that I called is that Mom and Dad are dead."

She was quiet for a few minutes. He gave her time. His sister might be a hot head and about the most beautiful woman in the world, but she didn't empty her head when there was reflecting to do.

"Who told you this?" He explained what Mr. Prince had told him, even about the way they'd not liked them. "Did I ever tell you that Mrs. Prince took me to the hospital a couple of times? She was the nicest person I ever knew. I was sorry to hear of her passing. What do you want me to do, Randy, other than piss on their graves?"

"That's what Tyler said you'd do. He's going with me, to settle up on anything that we might need to do. There is a lot of property there. I know that while it didn't grow shit, it was a good bit." She told him how many acres, then asked

15

him what would happen to it now. "I haven't any idea, to be honest with you. I don't know if there is a will or anything. It would be like them to think that they would live forever."

"Are they really dead, Randy? Please don't tell me this if it's not true. You of all people know what they did to me." He told her again, for like the millionth time, how sorry he was for everything. "It's not like you could have done anything about it. No one could have. They were out to kill us, or simply maim us in any way they could. I think they did a bang up job of it too."

"They're dead, honey. I promise you. Mr. Prince was the one that called, as I said, and he'd never lie to us about anything like that." She said nothing, but he could hear her heavy sigh. "I was going to ask you if you wanted to go there with Tyler and I. But I can understand if you don't want to go."

"I don't know." Again, Randy told her that he understood. "Can I let you know when you leave? You know me, because of my job, I have to be ready at a minute's notice. If not, then that's all right as well."

"I have to make arrangements for Tyler to go. And since we'll be staying overnight, I'll see about accommodations." She told him that she'd pay her part. "I have it this time. If something happens, then you can catch it the next. Or you can buy me dinner. Do you suppose Deb still works at the All Nighter?"

"I just bet that she does. I think she and her husband are older than our parents. And they have the best open faced sammiches I've ever eaten. Oh, now I'm hungry for one. And their pork fried sammiches. Holy shit, Randy—if I don't go, you'll have to bring those back with you."

He didn't know how that was going to work, but he'd give it his best shot. None of his sisters or brother ever asked for anything. So when they did, any of them, he went out of his way to get it for them.

After telling her he'd wait on her call, he called his wife, who was a teacher at the local high school. She wouldn't want to go either, only because she was coming up on her due date in a couple of months, but the doctor had already warned her about sitting in one place too long.

"I hope Meggie and Harper both go with you. Perhaps I'll give Meggie a call. You all need this, to finalize things." Randy told Alice that he didn't know if there was anything to finalize. "No, silly. I meant to have closure. I think you would sleep better, and I know that Meggie still has nightmares. Harper? Well, I know she's haunted, but she won't talk about it. And your brother...well, he has his own demons, doesn't he?"

"Yes. I think you're right. You talk to Meggie, and I'll arrange things for the four of us to go. I'll miss the kids and you." She said that she'd be right there when he returned. "All right, love, you work your magic and I'll work on this end of things. I love you, Alice Anne."

"And I love you Randy Panda."

He knew it was silly, the pet names, but he also knew that whenever the chance came up to do it, he was going to call her pet names until they were parted from this earth.

17

Chapter 2

Bryant wondered what there was to talk about with the Wilsons' will. But then, he'd never been one to pry into other peoples' business. It's why he hated when people messed with his. Taking a seat in the attorney's office made him nervous, but he was there for his dad, who had been called away by another matter.

"Mr. Prince?" He told the man he was Bryant. "Yes, your father told me who to expect. I have to tell you, I forgot completely that the Wilsons were a client of this firm. Even after their kids left home, thank goodness, they didn't come in and change things. Of course, my dad took care of their personal matters. It's hard to believe that they both died in that fire. Have you heard anything else about it?"

"No. Not as yet." Bryant knew that it was arson. He also knew that the fire marshal had reason to think that Mr. Wilson was dead before the fire started, and that Mrs. Wilson had started it. But he'd not speak out of turn. First of all, it wasn't anyone's business what happened except the Wilson

19

children's, and he wasn't going to be one to spread things before the facts were known. "You heard from the Wilson children, then?"

"Yes. Harper, the youngest, called me just this morning. She's difficult to get in touch with, I guess." Bryant had no idea. He'd heard of the children, but he'd never met them. The Wilsons had not been ones to socialize, nor had they allowed their kids to be out of their sight. "All right. I've read over the will that they had, and it's mostly outdated. They do mention all their children in it, what they're supposed to get, but it also mentions that they're to become wards of the state if their aunt, Michelle Wilson, on their father's side, is still alive. I have checked, and she is. So, although she is an immediate relative of the children, since they are grown adults, I will have to see them all to talk over what sort of things they'd like done with the land. That will be about the only thing that I can think that I'd have to personally discuss with them. Can you let them know when they arrive?"

"Yes, of course. My pops has been handling all of this, so I'll let him know. What does that, if anything, have to do with them now? I mean, they're no longer children, as you stated. Will the aunt have to be here as well? From what I understand, they might not like her any better than they did their parents." Bass, Mr. Townhouse, said that she'd have to be notified of their deaths, but that was all she'd been left, and that she no longer had any say over the adults. "I see. I'm to make sure that they're not going to be liable for anything concerning their parents' deaths."

"No. They paid their taxes every year. Never late. They had no credit cards that I could find. No credit in town, nor any kind of loans. They didn't have a car, as you might remember, and as far as valuables, I believe that everything in the house is gone." Bryant showed him the funeral bill, as well as the amount of produce that they'd sold off for the family. "That's a good bit, Bryant. Thank your family for me. There will be a little left over from this, and whatever is left, I was told by Randy to make sure that your family got it."

"That's not necessary. It was our pleasure to help them." Bass said nothing, but Bryant knew that the money was going to be given to them somehow. "I'm to understand from my pops that the kids are coming here. All of them."

"Yes. I heard from Randy, and he said that they had some things that they needed to do here. I think— If I'm honest with you, Bryant, I think they're here to make sure that they're gone. That was a terrible family. Just terrible." He'd heard some of the things about them, and about his mom taking the youngest to the hospital when her feet had been burned. "Anyway, I've asked Deb to make up some roast beef for those open faced sandwiches that she's so famous for."

It was one of his favorites as well. Not that he ate out much, but he did like a good sandwich when Deb made it. Getting all the information that Bass had, Bryant made his way to his place of work.

Bryant worked in a call center for a cable company. He was good enough at it that his bonus checks each month were bigger than his entire month of checks. And when they had contests, which wasn't all that often anymore, he would win at those too. It wasn't a great job, but it helped with the bills around the house. Last year they'd been able to put a much needed roof on the house and barn.

Bryant loved that they'd gone with a metal roof. It was his favorite sound of all times, he thought, being inside the barn

21

or up in his room when it was raining. The pitter patter of the rain hitting the tin made a sound that was like music to him. He'd almost be willing to sleep in the barn, where the noise was the best, for the rest of the summer just to hear it.

Sitting at his desk an hour later—he'd gotten there a little early today—he started answering his phone without thinking about anything going on around him. He had all the fixes down pat, and he was really good at upselling his customers. Also, and everyone that worked with him knew it, Bryant was very good at cooling tempers when it was necessary. Sometimes, and it was happening more often over the last few weeks, he'd be taking a call that was meant for the manager when she was "too busy" to be bothered.

Tonight he was going to train a new person, and as soon as the man sat down with him, Bryant knew that he would never make it. It wasn't a job for everyone. But the man pulled out his cell phone and watched it instead of listening to Bryant. It wasn't until Bryant told him he could take the next call that he stopped looking at the stupid thing.

"But I don't know what I'm doing. They said that I'd train for a week before I had to take my own calls." Bryant told him this was his call, and he'd be right there with him. "You take this one and I'll pay attention this time. I swear it."

Not only did he not pay attention, but he started texting someone on his phone even before Bryant was taking the next call. Glancing at the bright light of the phone, Bryant could see that the man thought him a dumbass if he thought he was going to ever take any kind of calls. He was there for management, apparently.

This went on for the next hour. Bryant wasn't pissed—he rarely lost his temper—but he wasn't going to be training this guy if this kept up. Getting up when he had a break, Doug, he thought his name was, went out to smoke and Bryant found his manager.

"Oh Bryant, just do it, will you? I have enough on my mind with trying to buy a house. Do you have any idea how frustrating it is or how much crap they want you to have?"

He didn't, but didn't answer her. Instead, he found himself a phone and called her boss. It was all he had left; the job was getting out of hand in reference to getting any help from her. Or for that matter, anyone else in the place. Some nights he felt like he was the only one working there.

"Mark, this is Bryant Prince. I'm having some issues here. I'm sorry to bother you at home, but I can't seem to get any help with my trainee."

Mark Shaw wasn't a great boss, but he was better than most. But when he told him to hang on a minute after telling him what Doug was doing, as well as what was told to him by Marie, he put him on hold. When he came back, Bryant was ready to tell him to forget it when he spoke first.

"All right, Bryant, I'm shadowing her computer now. I've had complaints about Marie lately, but when it comes from you, I put stock in it. Yes, by God, she is looking at homes. And on the chat with them. Christ, will no one work at their job they get paid for?" Bryant wasn't sure what he was supposed to say, so didn't say anything. "I'm coming in right now. Don't tell anyone, please. I don't have to worry about you not doing your job, never that. But heads are going to roll." The line was quiet, and he thought he'd hung up until Mark spoke again. "You think about taking her job for me, Bryant. I'll even make sure you make more than you did weekly, as well as bonuses. You're a good man."

"Thank you." But it went unheard because Mark had hung up.

At five minutes before his break was over, Bryant went back to his desk and set up for the rest of the night. He never drank soft drinks, but had a case of water under his desk. He knew that others sometimes took some of it, but he didn't mind, because most of the time they'd put some money on the desk for him. A couple of times he'd been left a nice gift of a book or something.

When his phone was ready to take calls, he realized that Doug was talking to one of the other people that worked with him, and Bryant didn't bother reminding him that he had a job. He wasn't a babysitter.

An hour later Bryant looked up from his screen. Doug was with him, but he was sound asleep in his chair with his headphones on, listening to music. Marie's door was open, which meant that she'd not left early yet. Taking his headphones off for a moment, Bryant could hear shouting from her office. Mark had made good on his threat.

An hour later Bryant was called to the office.

"You told him that I didn't have time to help you?" He wouldn't lie, no, but he didn't like someone telling on him without warning. "Christ, Bryant, just because you don't have a life doesn't mean that the rest of us don't."

He looked for Mark, and was upset that he seemed to be gone. But Marie was in full swing of telling him off, even going so far as to fire him. Bryant was headed back to his desk when Mark came out of the bathroom. He asked him what had happened.

"No, I'd never do that to someone. I didn't tell her. But she knew. She's got herself some snitches here that I'm going to take care of as well. Will you take the job?" Would he? Bryant told him that he'd not given it any thought. "Well, you finish up tonight, and when I come back in tomorrow, you can give me your answer. Oh, and I have fired about half the crew tonight, including Marie and Dougie boy. He said that you'd never said a word to him, so he took a nap."

"I tried to train him." Mark said that he knew that as well. "Mark, if I take this job, and I'm not saying that I will, I'm going to hold you to what you said before. My family and I can't handle a hit of me getting a promotion to only make less money. You understand that. And if it's not possible, then I can understand that as well."

"I said that I would and I will. I'd actually be saving money, because you'll have my back and make sure that things are going according to plan." Bryant said nothing else. Made no promises either. This man had been in charge and had complaints from people. So why hadn't he done something before tonight? "Bryant, what do you say you work for me as manager, and I'll make sure that your checks are taken care of?"

Alarms went off in his head. He didn't trust that this man would do anything he said. That he thought Bryant was so desperate to do what Mark wanted, that Bryant would do the job and be strung along for a while, with no money to compensate him. Shaking his head, Bryant backed out of the little office.

"No. I can't do that. You fix this up first—you know, with a contract like you had with the other managers—and I'll have my attorney go over it." Bryant no more had an attorney than he did the money to get one. "Since you have things under control now, I'll just get back to my desk and work out my shift. All right?"

Bryant didn't wait for an answer. He moved to his desk and noticed that not only was Doug gone, but his chair had been moved. As soon as he sat down, Mark came and sat down at his desk with him.

For a while, at least ten minutes, neither of them said anything to each other. Bryant answered several calls, upgraded two customers to a better package with some of the premium channels, and did a bill collection. Before his phone rang again, Mark put his phone on hold so that he'd not get any more calls. Bryant was waiting for the other shoe to drop.

~*~

Harper loved to run. It was the only way that she could stay fit when she wasn't working. But there were people around, a lot of them, and she couldn't take much of anymore. Harper would rather mess with a Bengal tiger than she would a single person. Even her family was getting on her nerves already.

Stopping at the edge of town, she walked up the drive to her parents' house to cool down. There was still a wall standing, but everything else was gone. She wondered if they'd ever gotten a car or something to drive at all, but looking into the still standing garage, she could see that it was as empty as she remembered it being when she'd been locked inside.

If anyone had come by the house when they were children, she would be the one that was locked in the garage. To say that it was as simple as that was wrong. She'd been chained to the walls like they had done to prisoners a long time ago. It was a threat to the others to make sure they kept their mouths shut when someone came to the door.

Harper knew that her brothers and sister wouldn't have done anything to get her into trouble. But there would always be some sort of infraction that they'd done that would get her beaten. Or worse yet, hung out there with only her toes touching the ground for a few days. As she'd gotten taller, the shackles would get moved up so that she wasn't able to ever touch the ground with her feet.

The shackles, she could see, were still there, and she wondered if anyone that had come here for the fire had remarked on them. Touching one with her finger, she felt all the hatred that she'd always felt when she thought of her parents. But today, it was doubled, simply because she was right here where some of her worst nightmares that still haunted her were. Harper turned around, and stopped in her tracks when there sat a large tiger.

"Shifter or real? I suppose if you were real, you'd not be able to answer me." The big black tiger laid down on the ground with his huge head on his paws. "Black tigers are rare; did you know that? I've only seen a few of them in my work. Will you be naked if you shift?"

He nodded, only lifting his head for a moment before he laid back down. Harper started forward to leave the garage, but he stood up. When she realized that he wasn't going to allow her to leave, Harper looked at the shackles again.

"They would hang me here when I was a kid. It wasn't really for anything that would warrant this kind of treatment, but they did it. Daily." She looked back at him. "If I promise not to run, will you allow me to exit here? This place gives me nightmares. Well, I have nightmares about living here, but this room is what we called the house of horrors as kids."

The big tiger stood up and she moved by him. When he

snapped at her hand she cried out, but didn't jerk from his massive teeth. It wasn't until she was released that Harper realized he'd done it so that he could speak to her.

I'm sorry. Not about your loss. From what I've heard, they should have died a long time ago. She nodded and moved out of the garage. The tiger followed her step by step. *My name is Bryant Prince. You must be Harper Wilson.*

"Yes, that's me. The youngest child of Randal and Margaret Wilson. Did you know them? Randal and Margaret?" Bryant said that he had not. "I came here today to see if it was true. I left here when Randy turned eighteen. I was hurt, and once I was released from the hospital that last time, he gathered us up and we took off."

I've spoken to your parents' attorney, Mr. Townhouse—yesterday, as a matter of fact. He still needs to meet with you all. You have an aunt. Did you know that? She said that she did know her, that Michelle Wilson was her name. *Yes, he did tell me that she was to have custody of you all in the event that your parents died before you were old enough. But there are things he still needs to go over.*

"He called the hotel this morning. I don't suppose you're from around here. I hate being in a hotel. Well, to be honest, I hate being around people. I'd rather—" Harper laughed. "Believe it or not, I was thinking just as I was walking up here that I'd rather tangle with a large tiger than people. I was thinking Bengal, but I guess I had no idea that there were any tigers around here."

We're a special kind of tiger. My family was the first black tigers. And we're not really shifters, however. We were tigers first, then the lady of the earth changed us into humans. I guess right after we were born. She asked him how many there were. *Counting*

28

my father, Buck Prince, there are seven of us. My mom passed away some time ago.

Harper wasn't anxious to get away from Bryant. Usually she could be counted on to have a short conversation with someone, then be on to something else. But when she leaned back on the grass that hadn't been scorched by the fire, he laid his big head on her belly. Harper began running her fingers through his fur as she spoke again.

"The week before we left here, I was in the house of horrors. I'd been sent there the day before, and had to stand up in one place until they came out and gave me my punishment. If I moved, or laid down, I would get double the punishment from them." She continued to pet him as she thought of what they'd done to her. Bryant told her to go on. "I don't remember now what it is that was done. It didn't have to be me that did anything. For some reason they would target all their anger on me. Now, years later, I think it was because I'd never give into whatever they were doing to me. I didn't scream, nor did I beg. Tyler learned very early — fat lot of good it did him — that begging would give them what they wanted, and it would make the pain shorter."

You're strong. I can tell that by the way you're gripping my fur. She let him go and he laughed. Harper felt it all the way to her backbone. His laughter even made her smile. *I know this will sound like a sappy statement, but think about it. You'd not be what and who you are today without what they did to you. I'm not saying that it was right — never that — but you are a strong minded person. Only someone as strong as you would have been able to come out here and be inside of the place where you were hurt most.* Harper had heard that before, but for some reason it meant more coming from this man, who wasn't getting paid to talk

29

to her. *Go on with your tale. I want you tell me.*

"All right. But I am going to warn you, my parental units were not warm and fluffy. I really do have nightmares every night because of them." He said he was sorry, and encouraged her to go on. Again the fact that she could talk to this man so easily astonished her. "I had fallen down at some point in the night, badly enough that I had knocked myself unconscious. I know that because the doctor told me at my last hospital visit here that I had a recent concussion. They didn't take me to the hospital—no, Randy did. And once I was there, I vowed never to return."

How old were you, Harper? She had to think. Back then, birthdays hadn't meant shit to anyone. When she told him, he sat up and looked at her. *You were only twelve? Christ. Pops said that my mom took you to the hospital once. Please don't tell me you got into trouble for that.*

"It's all right. If she'd not gotten me help then I wouldn't have survived that day." She closed her eyes, thinking about what no person should ever endure. "I had fallen. I really was weak and hurting, and I was told that they'd have their justice for me embarrassing them. I'm not sure how that was working, but I knew better than to say a word. The fire was started on the floor, just inside the doors. One of them had shackled me up to the wall. And while the fire was being stoked, Margaret was using the baseball bat on my body, mostly my ribs. She loved hearing them break when she was pissed off. Then while my father was getting the branding iron hot enough to— What is it?"

He had stood up so quickly that she felt her heart race and her muscles tighten in anticipation. While she didn't see anything, looking in the direction he was, she was very still, not trying to act like she knew any more than he did.

"Bryant?" He told her to be still for a moment. He was trying to figure out if the male was alone. Now speaking in a whisper, she asked if it was human or not. She didn't get an answer.

Before she could move, even if she thought to, Bryant had leapt. She was sure that he hadn't meant to knock her backwards, but she ended up on her ass. Harper watched the two animals fighting. One of them was Bryant, the other a great gray wolf, and his size told her that he was an alpha—and stupid.

Bryant was twice his size and meaner, it looked to her. Even when the wolf realized that he was defeated, Bryant kept at him, tearing into his flesh until he was nothing more than a whimpering animal. When Bryant looked as if he was going to go on the attack again, Harper stood in front of the big tiger.

"Enough. The lesson is taught. Whatever the fuck you were trying to teach him, he's got it. Back off. I promise you, if he comes at you again, I will kill his fucking ass. It's the least that he deserves." The wolf took off, limping and holding up one of his front paws. Turning back to Bryant when the wolf was gone, she was suddenly on her back, his big body over hers. "What the hell are you doing? I do not find this to be the least bit sexy, you moron. Besides that, you have blood all over your...whatever you call that mug of yours. Face? Fur ball? Whatever. It's not sexy either."

The tiger was gone, and the man that she knew the tiger had been was atop her. Not struggling, Harper just looked at Bryant's face while he stared down at her. There was something about him, a thing that she couldn't put her finger

31

on at the moment, that intrigued her. And for the first time in her life, Harper knew she was safe.

"Finish the story please." Harper didn't know what he meant, what he was talking about. Her mind was elsewhere, like on his body pressing hard into hers. "Tell me what they did to you. You said he was heating up the branding iron. What did he do to you?"

"He got it hot enough. White hot. I remember thinking that as soon as it touched my skin it was going to melt into me and I'd be disfigured for the rest of my life. And at the time, I thought that it would have been preferable if I had just let them kill me." Bryant only said no, but it was hard, like it would not be rebuked. "He burned it to the bottom of my feet—it was the letter W, for whore, he told me. And as I lay there, my feet burnt to the bone, my body broken and battered, he stood over me and pissed all over me."

Bryant kissed her. It was savage, painful, and consuming. Harper wrapped her legs around him, feeling the length of his cock as he pressed more and more into her. When he slid his mouth down over her throat, she let him have it. Anything he wanted, she realized, she'd give him. And when he bit her, tearing off her clothing at the same time, she came so hard that she screamed.

He entered her the same way he'd taken her mouth, possessing her with his body and mouth. And when he cried out her name, then threw back his head, Harper came as well. It was epic, and more than she could take. So when she blacked out, Harper's last thought was that she wasn't going to be harmed again.

Chapter 3

Bryant sat on the ground and waited for her to wake. His mate. As soon as he had entered the garage, her scent was all over the place. Other scents as well, but hers had called to him. Looking at his brother as he pulled into the driveway of her home, he saw Samson put the bag from Bryant's car down on the ground and leave.

Samson wouldn't tell anyone what he'd done, nor would he tell the reason that Bryant had needed him for something. It would be up to him to do that. Not that he wasn't looking forward to having a mate, but Bryant didn't have a house. Not to mention, he didn't even have a room of his own at his parents' house.

There hadn't been the money for any of them to move out on their own. He supposed that he could have—any of them could have—but it was cheaper, he knew, for them all to live in the house that was not only paid for, but his family was there as well.

Bryant didn't mind being nude. He was a cat first and

33

foremost. With the magic he had, it would have been easy to dress them both. But as this was their first of everything, he didn't want to freak her out more.

As he made his way down the drive to his clothing, he kept an eye out for the alpha. He hadn't any idea what had made him attack today, but he was going to have a word with the alpha that was in charge of the pack here. Bryant would bet anything that he hadn't any idea that the other wolf was around.

Picking up the duffle, he read the note that was attached to the top. "Congratulation, big brother." Smiling, he pulled out a pair of shorts and pulled them on. He might not care if he was naked or not, but Harper might.

Harper. He even loved her name. Laughing out loud, he saw her head come up off the ground and her look directly at him. Still a few feet away, he asked her if she was all right. It just occurred to him that she might not have cared that he'd taken her.

"Just fine. And you?" He said he'd never felt better. "Yes, well, I was going to say that, but didn't want to give you a big head. Christ, that was incredible. I've never enjoyed anything as much as I did that."

"I was afraid that I might have hurt you." She took the duffle from him, reading the note but not commenting. "I'm sorry about your clothing. I was in a hurry to have you."

"Yes, well, you might have noticed that I didn't fight you off all that much." She pulled his shirt over her head, getting her hair all tangled around the buttons. As he was helping her out of it, she turned and looked at him. "I'm assuming, and this might just be me, but that we're mates. That was why it was so mind blowing."

"What if I told you I was that mind blowing all the time?" She smacked him on the chest and looked in the bag again. "Yes, you're my mate. I knew that someone here was. I could smell them, but the scent was old, and I had no idea if it had been someone just passing through."

They started walking back after he found her a pair of shorts that cinched up. He didn't know what to say. As usual, Bryant wasn't much of a talker. When their hands touched, he held onto hers, curling his fingers around them. Thinking about his night last night, he decided to tell her just how unable he was to afford anything right now. Not that she had asked.

"I worked for the cable company as a customer service rep until last night. It was a good job, paid me well, but only because of the bonus checks that I got." She looked at him and smiled. "The reason I'm mentioning this is because it was pointed out to me, just before I was fired, that I'm a fucking idiot for working in a kid's job."

"Your boss?" He nodded. "I did that for a little while. Making my way in the world so I could survive. Then I found a camera in a second hand shop. My life sort of took on a new meaning then. Why did this jackass call you that and fire you?"

"I wouldn't take over the position of manager. He said that he'd make sure that I got my bonus money in addition to my regular checks. I made great money on the bonus — usually twice as much as my regular checks. So his promise was that if I took the job now, without the pay raise, he'd make sure I got it. And when I asked about having that in writing, he fired me." Harper told him she didn't think that was legal. "Legal or not, I'm out of a job. And I'm betting that

35

he'll find some way to make sure that I'm not paid either."

"Bastard." She picked up her cell phone out of the mailbox at the end of the driveway. "I haven't any idea why I did that when I got here. I think it was because I didn't want to be tempted to take any pictures with it. I have enough memories of this place to last me several lifetimes. Will I be staying with you now?"

"You can if you don't mind sharing a room with Samson and me on a twin bed." She laughed, and he told her he was serious. "There hasn't been a lot of money in our family. We make do, barely, but it's never going to see us getting rich. I'll get us an apartment, but it won't be fancy."

"I have a house. A condo too." He didn't say anything, trying to think what that meant to him. Was she leaving him for better digs? "I have money too, Bryant. Not that I'm trying to say I'm better than you. But as a photographer, I'm making really good money from my pictures. Do you understand? I don't know what it's going to do for us to have my parents dead. But I'm sure there might have been a few dollars or so in the safe. Did they get it open?"

"Safe? I don't know. I mean, I wouldn't even know who to ask about that." He almost told her that he'd take care of their living arrangements, but honestly, he didn't have any way of doing that at all. "Harper, I'm a man without anything but my family. And for them, I'd do just about anything."

"That's wonderful. I'm glad that you love your family. And I think your parents would be people that I'd like to get to know. I mean, you're clean. You don't smell — well, not too badly anyway. And you've been nothing but polite since we met." She grinned at him. "I'm betting that your father is a good looking older man with graying hair. Right? And your mom, she used to keep him in line by tisking at him."

"You are right about my mom. I miss her every day. My dad is going to surprise you. I'm not sure what you know about shifters—a lot, I think—but we don't age like humans do. And being what we are, we haven't aged since we turned twenty-eight." She asked him just how old he was. "Just over fifteen hundred years old. My pops is older by twenty or so years."

Bryant walked a couple of more steps before he realized that she was no longer with him. He turned around quickly to see what had happened to her, ready to attack again, when she asked him if he was serious.

"Yes. I mean, I guess I could have worked our way up to that, but I didn't think about it. To be honest, I felt so comfortable with you that I— Are you all right?" She bent at her waist, allowing him a nice view of her breasts. But he was more concerned about her than about sampling her again. "I didn't mean to upset you."

"You didn't. I mean, you did, but not like you think." She looked at him. "You've aged incredibly well for an old geezer."

They laughed as he chased her through the fields where his family and the others had just taken the crops in. When he caught her, he let the impact of their fall hit him, and held her above him as he looked at her. She told him that they didn't have time for sex again.

"Why not?" She said she didn't know, but asked if he could just give her a moment. Nodding, he waited while she answered her cell phone when it rang. In the meantime, Bryant reached out for his dad. *I thought that I should tell you that I've met my mate. I haven't any idea what we're going to do or where we're going to live, but I wanted you to know that it's Harper Wilson.*

That's about the best news I've heard all day, son. That is just great. He told him about how she thought Buck was old. *Should I change me around or something? I can do that, you know.*

No. I want her to love you as much as we all do just the way you are.

His dad was quiet for a moment. *That boss of yours, he's called here a couple of times. Giving you a second chance, he said. I know that you needed to leave there, but this guy is coming unglued when I tell him you're not home. I'm expecting him to show up at any time about this. You did good to get yourself out of there, Bryant. Even if you were fired, I think you're better off. I'm not saying that you were, but I don't want to deal with him right now.*

His pops was dealing with other issues. The land taxes were coming due, and it was a little more than they had anticipated. Since Bryant no longer had a check coming in, that was going to put a pinch on things. There wasn't even enough money to pay for food this month if they didn't figure out something soon.

"I have to go." Bryant asked her if she wanted him to go with her. "I'd like that, yes. But don't feel obligated. I know that you're busy at home too."

"Not right now, no. And you come first." They stood up. "Where are we headed? If you don't mind me asking."

"The attorney. Mr. Townhouse said that he needs to speak with all of us concerning the will and the contents of it. I also mentioned the safe, and he said that it would be better if we have the police open it. That way there isn't any trouble later." He asked her if she thought there would be. "No, I don't. But then, you can never tell about Michelle. She's always thought that my parents were never hard enough on us. I don't think she saw the real them. Or if she really did believe that, then she's nuttier than they were."

They went into the hotel that her family was staying at so she could change too. Bryant had stopped at his home to do the same before coming here. Bryant hadn't realized that Tyler was in a wheelchair, nor did he know that Meggie was missing her left hand. He hadn't any idea why, but he would bet it was because of the parents. Taking Tyler down in the elevator, Bryant asked if he wanted him to push him to the meeting or if he wanted to be in a car.

"You don't mind pushing me?" Bryant said it would be his pleasure. That he could point out some improvements around town that had been happening of late. "I lived here when I was younger, you know. But since I've been in this thing, I don't get around much. I, too, was rescued by Randy when we left town. I was in a home, however."

"The more I find out about your parents, the more and more I wish I had known them so that I could have killed them before now." Bryant stopped when Tyler asked him if he was serious. "Yes."

"Wow, I wish I had known you when I was younger."

They were at the attorneys' offices by then, and he picked the younger man up and carried him into the office. There wasn't any room for the chair in the office. Plus, it wasn't any hardship for Bryant to carry him.

"I believe that I could like having you around, Bryant. But sadly, I'm going to leave when my family does. I live with Meggie for now. She needs help just coping with life most of the time. She and I, we didn't suffer as much as Harper did, but we did have our issues too."

39

"I'm assuming that you're in the wheelchair because of them." Bryant didn't mention that he and Harper were mates and he'd be wherever she was. It was obvious to him that there was nothing for her here. He didn't even own a house. "And your sister? She lost her hand because of them too?"

"I was in the back seat of a van with all of them. I haven't any idea where we were coming from, but we'd been prettied up, Meggie calls it, and warned that we were to say nothing and do nothing to embarrass them. Not that it mattered — they always thought we were the worst of children. Usually Harper would pay. But I'm getting side tracked." He grinned at Bryant, and Bryant found himself liking the man. "I had to pee. I mean, like go so bad I hurt from it. When I asked if we could perhaps pull over, they did. Imagine my surprise when Margaret got out of the van and let me unbuckle. But before I could get out, Randal pulled forward at a high rate of speed, like fifty or so, and Margaret threw me from the open door. I hit the road and grass on my back and broke it."

"Christ." Tyler nodded. "I'm so very sorry, Tyler. Seriously, had any of us known, we would have rescued you. We didn't know."

"No one did. I mean, when we were out in public — never in town, however — we were a picture perfect family, all neatly dressed, hair all combed and trimmed. Our clothing was just long enough or loose enough to cover any bruises or wounds. But when we got home, they'd make us undress, then pick one of us to go to the house of horrors. And as I said before, it was usually Harper." Bryant asked why it was usually her. "I don't know. I'm not sure any of us knew. She was the youngest, but even that didn't explain why she was the target of most of what went on. I mean, they didn't do

40

those things to me when I was the youngest child."

When everyone was gathered together, Harper told them what he was to them. Tyler was very excited, and Randy hugged him several times. Whatever he'd expected to happen in the way of welcoming him to their family, this wasn't it. Meggie was a little reserved, but she did smile at him. And when Townhouse came into the room, he didn't ask at all why he was there.

~*~

Harper looked over the land rights. They were not signed over to any of them, according to the paperwork from the attorney, which was both good and bad. Whoever was to take it would have had a great deal of land. And if none of them wanted it, the little town would change a great deal, because someone would purchase it for something ugly and huge. Not even Michelle had been given the land rights, as Bass thought she would have been. He told them that because the children weren't mentioned in the will, nor had they given the land away, it would be divided up between the four of them.

"I don't want it." She looked over at Randy, and he shook his head. "I want nothing to do with it. No money that might come from the sale of it. I'll never come back here and be nostalgic about it. Nothing. I would very much like for you to divide the land up between the other three. I'm finished with this after we leave here."

"Mr. Wilson, the land proceeds alone could pay off a great amount of money if it were sold. Even the fourth that you'd own." Randy just told him no, he did not want it. "What about you three? Would you be willing to take his quarter without question?"

"I don't want it either. It wouldn't bother me the least bit if

41

it sat there and went back to whatever it was before they built out there. Like Randy, I'm never coming back here." Meggie looked at Bryant as she continued. "I'm sorry. I know that you live here, and you might even be proud of your town. But I'm not. I don't want it. Tyler can build him a house and live out here with Harper if he wants, but not me. It's—"

"I go where you are, Meggie. We need each other." Meggie reached for Tyler's hand and held it tightly. They had formed a sort of wounded family, the two of them. Harper looked at Bryant when Tyler spoke again. "They're a couple, Harper and Bryant. I'm willing to sign my part over to them, to make it a happier place, if the rest of you would. She deserves it anyway."

"I won't take this because you feel sorry for me." Tyler threw back his head, and Harper felt her temper get the better of her. "Listen, bub. You know as well as I do that you suffered at their hands worse than me. I can at least walk."

"You can. All of you can. But that's not what had me laughing. I was just thinking about you, of all the kids living there, building a happy home on the land, raising up a bunch of kids, and being as happy as they were only when they hurt us." Tyler looked at her hard. "Take the land. All of it if they're willing. And make it a place that it never was, Harp. A place that sings with laughter, happiness, and family. A place where a family could enjoy holidays and birthdays. Hell, you do that, you make it a place that is nothing like it was, and I promise you, I'll come to see you every summer. Every holiday, just so I can bask in the irony of it all."

Both Meggie and Randy were nodding at her.

"You'd come to see me too? You'd visit me if I took this and made it into my home?" Meggie said that she would, but the house would have to be in a different spot. "I'd do that, only to build closer to Bryant's family. They're very close. I might have to take a few ideas from them on how to be a normal family. But yes, I'd do that. And anytime you wanted it back, all you'd—"

Randy cut her off by looking at Townhouse. "Can you write up a contract for each of us, saying that we willingly give the land to Harper at no cost to her, no give backs? We'd have no ties to it whatsoever other than to come and see her." Bass asked if he wanted that in there. "All but the visiting part. I will do it, but I have my own family now, and I'll have to talk to them about the holidays. But yes, we want it drawn up so that she has it."

"All right. I'll do that and have it to you all in a couple of days." Bass put the paperwork away that was about the land. "I'll file it for you each as well, and have you a copy of it. Now, we need to talk about the safe in the basement that Harper knew about. Did the rest of you?"

"Yes, but if it's filled with anything of value, my thoughts on it are the same as the land. I don't want it. As far as I'm concerned, it's blood money. Our blood money. Harper can have mine to build with."

Harper stood up. "Wait. This is going too fast for me. All right, I can understand the land. I was going to say the same thing, I didn't want it, but I found Bryant—or he found me—and we will need a place to live. But this safe? You guys remember that sucker. It's fucking huge." Her family nodded. "Look. Just see what's in it. Please. I'd feel better about you giving the land to me if you first take a look at what else was left behind."

"No." Meggie stood up and asked Bryant if he could help

43

her once again with Tyler. She was leaving, and didn't want anything to do with the land or the money. When Bryant stood up to help with Tyler, Harper asked her where she was going. "I love you with all my heart, Harper, and I will for the rest of my days. I know what you did for us, protecting us from our parents. You saved the rest of us from being hurt as much as you were. I know that."

"How could you know such a thing?" Meggie opened her purse and pulled out an envelope. Then she handed it to her. "What is this?"

"Every time I was caught at something, every single time after you were old enough to walk, a tally was written up. I guess you could say it was from Margaret, but it was about you and me. Look at one of them." Harper didn't want to, but Bryant took it from her and pulled out the very top note. "It says, 'I know you used a quarter cup of laundry detergent too much today. Harper said she did it.' I wanted to hate you for that, for being the martyr. But then I noticed something else, something that we all noticed after we thought about it. You didn't just to it for me, you did it for all three of us. All the time. And you never, not one time, asked for anything in return. Honey, I love you, Harp."

"I love you guys too. But I'm sure you have it wrong." But Tyler handed her his envelope, then Randy. Each note listed something they'd done that Harper had taken the heat for. "Where did you get these? I had no idea she was telling you this."

"She didn't. I found them the night that we left—the day that they burned you to the point where we all thought you'd die. They were out there with you, and I knew that we had to get away or die. So I looked for money and found those."

Randy got up and hugged her. "I have no idea when they were going to give them to us. I don't care. But the fact that they knew and that you did it makes me want to give you everything you never had when we were children, just to...I don't know. Just to thank you for everything."

Harper looked up after reading every one of the little transgressions. There was even something written on the back of them about how they had punished her. Her brothers and sister were gone, leaving her and Bryant there alone. She asked him when they'd left.

"Not long ago. About an hour." She told him that was a long time. "Not to me. Not to see every emotion that you felt racing over your face. The pain that tore through you with every individual reading. To see you deal with each of those slips of papers a great deal better than I ever would have."

She gathered them all up and put them back into their envelopes. "I want us to build a house. And once the fireplace is in, the Christmas tree is up and decorated with things we like—the house and the tree—I want to have my family back so that we can burn these in the fireplace and have a party."

"All right." He stood up and stretched. "Bass is going to take us out to the safe with the police. My brothers will be there too, to lend a hand in getting it out of the sublevels. Fisher said that he has located it in the basement, but it won't come out easily."

"You think that—? Never mind. You can get it out of there. I have a single favor to ask of you." Bryant told her that he'd do anything for her. "Thank you. But you should hear this first. I travel a great deal. I mean, I have enough travel miles to go around the world several times. But I don't want you to work. I want you to be there with me every time

45

I go someplace new. I don't know that I've felt this safe, this secure, with anything in my life. And it's all because of you."

"Deal. And I have to tell you something, Harper. I've fallen in love with you. I don't know how we're going to make it in this life, but we will, because we have each other. Too sappy?"

She wasn't sure what love felt like, not for someone that you wanted to spend your life with. She loved her family, but of course that wasn't nearly the same. But Bryant seemed to understand, and they moved out of the room.

Bryant didn't say anything more, but she could almost touch his emotions. He was worried. About what, she had no idea, but she'd find out, and she'd do her best to fix it for him. As they were going out the door, he told her they could walk again if she wanted, or they could ride with his pops.

"His truck is full of junk right now, things he's been meaning to sell off. But it runs good." She said she owned a car that she'd have brought here. "That could be expensive."

They were going to have to talk, she and he. There were a great many things she was going to have to explain to him and let him know about. Bryant, and his family by extension, were no longer poor. Because she wasn't.

"I don't care if his truck is as many colors as a blanket—I don't mind at all." He was laughing as they walked out into the afternoon sunline. "Oh Bryant, I can't tell you how happy I am that you found me. I know that seems really odd, coming from someone that just met you. But I already know that you're going to be the best for me, and with me."

Buck pulled up just as she was looking for a place to sit down. She wasn't tired, but she wanted to enjoy the sunshine on her face for a little while longer. When he got out of his truck, which had a great many colorful pieces holding it together, Harper got a hug like none other. She felt it to her toes.

"I already love you, child. The happiness that you've brought to this family is just what we all needed. Bryant told me that you're going to be living right next door to us, too. Couldn't have been happier about anything other than you telling me you are breeding. Which, I know you're not." She asked him how that worked, and then answered her own question. "Yes, it's your scent. You're going to be a good mother, I think. And you couldn't do better with a mate like my boy here."

"He told me how old he is. I wasn't sure if he was joking or not." Buck said that she might want to remember that he could never lie to her. It was in their genes. "I think I knew that, but it's good to hear. Thank you, Buck. Let's go see what Mr. and Mrs. Wilson left us, all right?"

The trip was short, and she loved the fun that she'd been having with the patriarch of the family. Buck was funny, smart, and had a good head on his shoulders when it came to farming. She might just have to have him come and see what her and Bryant had in the way of land soon.

Chapter 4

Bryant saw Mark coming toward him just as they were getting the straps under the safe. It was large—heavy too. He figured that with it being about six feet by four by four, the thing had to weigh at least a couple of thousand pounds. That wasn't counting whatever was in it, either.

It had been his pop's idea to use the straps. The man from the company, Mr. Talbert, was there with paperwork. He needed to verify the serial number on the back, then he could give Harper the access code. None of the rest of her family was there.

"Okay, boys. Draw in a deep breath, let it out."

Pops did that twice more before he said to pull. The safe nearly toppled back into the hole when they got it to the top, but Mr. Talbert gave it that extra push and the safe landed on its side. Setting it up wasn't as difficult, but it did give them some trouble. Once it was in the right position, they were set to open it—once they had the combination.

"You guys did it. Pizza all around for dinner," Buck said.

After the serial numbers were identified, Mr. Talbert asked them what they were going to do with it now that the house was gone around it. Harper told him that it would depend on what was inside of it. He said that he understood and stepped back. That gave Mark the opening he'd been waiting for to corner Bryant.

"You given any thought to taking that job, Bryant?" He told him that he'd not thought of it once. "Not once? I thought you told me that you needed your income to make ends meet. Did I hear you wrong? Have you won the lottery and no one told me?" Mark laughed, but it wasn't very sincere sounding.

"First of all, why would I need to have you informed if I won anything? Second thing, you fired me. Simply because I wanted it in writing that you would pay me as you said that you would." Mark was shoved out of the way by Harper, and Bryant smiled at her. "Also, I don't think I'm coming back to work there at all. I might even retire and see the world."

"Yeah, sure you will. And I'll grow horns." Officer Herb Bonner came up and stood behind Mark. Herb asked if this man was bothering him. "We're talking about his job. Can we have a few minutes here?"

"He's busy, in the event you didn't notice. Now, you weren't invited out here for this thing, and I, for one, would like for you to move on. Or, and this would be my pleasure, I can move you on. Up to you." Mark turned to Herb and asked if he was serious. "I rarely have a sense of humor when it comes to assholes. So like I said, Mr. Shaw, move or I'll move you."

"I just want to know when Bryant is coming back to work." Harper stood between him and Mark. He hadn't any idea what she was doing, but he didn't tell her to move back.

"What? The little lady is going to fuck up my day? I don't think so. Get out of my way."

Mark only put his hands out. Bryant wasn't sure if he ever touched Harper, but she fell back into his arms like she'd been shoved hard. And when he asked her if she was all right, she winked at him and turned back to Herb. This was going to be good. His family was right there watching every move, too.

"He assaulted me." Mark said he'd not touched her. "Oh? Well, I guess that I fell backwards on my own. Officer Bonner, I'd like to press charges against this man. He pushed me. Had it not been for my fiancé, I would have fallen on my ass. I have so much going on right now."

She turned into Bryant's chest and sounded like her heart was broken when Harper started crying. If he wasn't this close to her, he would have sworn that she was really upset. As Mark was being hauled away, she held onto him and looked at his brothers and father.

"I learned that trick when I was in Indonesia. This guy, he was harassing me about my lack of luggage, and I couldn't handle him— Are you guys all right?" Bryant looked at his brothers. All of them seemed to be in the verge of shifting. "I'm not hurt, not at all. He really didn't even touch me. I just wanted him gone."

"We need to be able to know that." Harper nodded, and Kylan asked her if she knew what that meant. "I don't want you to think that we're going to know your every mood and movement. Not unless you're needing us."

"You take a part of my blood." Kylan nodded. "I'm sorry that I frightened you, or whatever it was that happened. But that guy had to go. He already fired your brother, for no reason other than his ego was as big as his dick is tiny."

51

Pops was the first to laugh, then the others. She was, Bryant thought, a breath of fresh air when it came to saying what she needed or wanted.

Mr. Talbert cleared his throat. "I have a check here for you, Ms. Wilson." She corrected him. "All right, Harper. The safe that your parents purchased was one of the first that was ever made. And with it came a stock option. I wasn't there when it was taken out for them, but I'm to understand that they wanted more. The stocks should have been given to them over a period of time—quarterly. But somehow it fell through the cracks. If you'd be so kind as to tell me who to make the check out to, then I can be on my way."

"Buck Prince." Pops stopped her by telling her no. Harper asked how much money he had charged for gathering up the families to bring in the crops. Pops said nothing. "Then I want the check to go to you. It might not be all that much, and you'll be able to pay for a movie to rent or something. But if it's enough, I'm hoping that it will take the worry lines off not only your face, but the rest of the men too."

"What if it's a great deal? I mean, it could be hundreds of dollars, honey. You might need it." She told the man to make the check out to Bryant's pops. "I don't know what to say. As you said, it might be a little, but it'll certainly come in handy."

Mr. Talbert was smiling when he handed the check over to Harper. When she only glanced at it, she too was smiling. She knew that Pops was going to lose their home if they didn't have some help.

Pops staggered back when he looked at the check. "It's too much." She said that as far as she was concerned, because of what his wife had done for her, it wasn't nearly enough. "Harper, you have no idea how much we wish we'd done more. Stepped in when it was obvious that you children weren't getting what you needed in the way of love and shelter. But we never knew about the rest of it. And when Sara took you to the hospital and you all ran, we were never so happy for anything in our lives."

They hugged. It wasn't like any other hug that Bryant had witnessed before — this one was of love, friendship, and also trust. Pops asked her if he could ask her a favor. Harper told him that he could forever ask her anything he wanted.

"If you need this money, you'll let me know. After I pay the taxes on the house, I'll put this away and you can come get it anytime you want. All you have to do is ask." She hugged him again, and then leaned back into Bryant's chest. Bryant held her tightly as she spoke again.

"I'm smart, Buck. Very much so. I invest low, sell high. I never buy anything unless I really need it or it's for work. Then I go all out with my camera equipment. Also, because of the fact that I can take pictures that no one else wants to, from animals to war zones, I get paid a great deal of money for my photos. I am — and now this would include Bryant — a millionaire several times over."

Bryant looked at his brothers, then at his dad. He wondered if their reaction to her announcement was the same on each of their faces.

"I'm sorry. I must have misheard you. Did you say that you were millionaires?" Harper nodded at Pop's question. Then she told him several times over. "You don't look like a millionaire. Not that I know anyone with that much money, but you look as down on your luck as we do."

"And that, my dear sir, is why I've never been taken advantage of. Besides, when I am — when some asshole thinks

53

that he's smarter than me, or stronger, I put him in his place right now and don't think another thing about it." She looked up at Bryant. "I wanted to tell you this earlier. Or even later tonight. I have already contacted my — our attorney, and you are on all my accounts. Whatever is in this thing, we're going to toss it all away or start fresh. Just as soon as we can get a contractor here to build for us."

"I don't care how much or how little you have." He kissed her then. "But I have to tell you, I'm relieved. When you were talking about a house we were going to have build, I was terrified that we were going to be in deep trouble. Even if we'd have gotten the house built, what were we going to do for furniture? I mean, you slept in my room last night. What did you think of sleeping on a single bed?"

"Believe it or not, I've slept in worse conditions. Once I was in the mountains, trying to get a good shot of the people that lived there. They deal with the outside world, but only a couple of the people — men — could leave the village and get the supplies. I caught a terrible cold, and one of the women, out harvesting the fresh snow for water, found me." Bryant asked her if she got the shot. "I did, as a matter of fact. A great many of them. The woman dragged me to her hut and warmed me up, and gave me some of her herbs. As I recuperated, I walked around the village and snapped shots of the everyday goings on of the women there. Most of the men, it turned out, were off hunting for goats that were higher up, and they hadn't returned as yet."

"You've had yourself a great many adventures, then?" She nodded at Marcus. "I'd love to see some of your pictures. I mean, if you don't mind sharing."

"No, I'd be honored to show them to you. But there are a

great many of them. I don't use digital all the time. I'm hooked on a regular camera that I can hold onto the shot when I'm finished. But you'll be happy to know that they are in albums, all marked as to where I took them. But as I said, there are even hundreds of those." She looked at him. "I'm sorry."

"Why on earth are you sorry? You, in one hour, have made my entire family want to die for you." Harper looked at his family, then back at Bryant when they were nodding that they would. "And someday, if you have a mind to, I'd like to marry you. Make you as much a part of this family legally as you already are in our hearts."

"Okay." Everyone laughed. Pops dug into his pocket and pulled out a long chain. He handed it to Bryant and kissed Harper on the cheek as he walked away. "This was your mother's, wasn't it?"

"Yes. She wore it every day after she was changed into a human. My dad couldn't afford much, but he bought her this ring by paying a little every week until he could get it for her." Taking the chain off, he bent on one knee. "Harper Wilson, will you consent to be my wife, to love me like no other? I will forever be yours. I already love you with all that I am. Please?"

"Yes. But you should give the ring back to your father when we marry." Bryant asked her why. "So that each of his sons can use it to ask the woman that they find to complete their lives."

It was only a plain band of gold, nicked and worn in places. There was a small cut down the middle of it that would stretch when his mom had shifted.

After placing the ring on her finger, Bryant kissed her, giving her all the passion he had stored up for her. When they pulled back to look at one another, he could see that she was happy. And to Bryant, that was worth everything in the world.

"Now, let's see what is in this sucker. Please, can one of you take pictures?" Fisher said he would record it all. "Thank you very much. I'd hate for us to find a body or something in there, and have the death blamed on me."

She was kidding, he thought. Then he thought of her parents, the things that he'd heard about them, the first-hand knowledge he had of them. Looking at the safe and then back at Harper, he was almost afraid for her to open it up.

~*~

Samson had brought boxes to put whatever was in the safe that was to be disposed of in them. The only thing that had ended up in them was cash, and a great deal of it. Thinking that there was some sort of magical hole or something in the safe, he thought that there was an endless supply of cash. There were Baggies of gems too. Some he knew by color. The rest, he only knew that they were pretty when the sun hit them just right.

There were other things as well. Books by authors that he hadn't heard of. Torture magazines that made him sick to touch them. Bondage items that hadn't been used, as well as a stack of books that looked like a kid's school notebooks. They were all dated and put in order.

A drawer at the bottom of the safe had a lock on it, but lucky for them, the key was hanging in the safe. When he opened it the ground shook, and he fell back on his ass. Whatever was in the black bag, the only thing in the drawer, it was powerful.

"Don't touch it. That is mine."

He looked up at Aurora. She was as beautiful as ever with her wings spread out behind her, the sun shining through them to cast sparkles all over the ground beside and behind him. But there was anger too. Not to mention, several million faeries with their arrows pointed at them that brought home that point quickly. "You have stolen from me, and I shall have my revenge."

No one moved. The faeries moved closer to them all as Aurora moved closer to the safe. He'd been wrong about her anger. She wasn't just mad, but pissed, and Samson thought that if any one of them so much as farted, they'd all be so full of the arrows there would be no coming back from it. He knew for a fact that the points were all covered in the deadliest poisons known to any creatures. Bryant told Harper that this was Aurora, queen of the lands.

"My lady, whatever you think we have done to wrong you, I swear to you that we'll make up for it. We've only just opened this up. My parents, you see, they were the ones that owned this." Aurora turned all her attention to Harper when she spoke. "Whatever is in this thing, I don't care if it's every last item in it, if you were robbed of it by them, then please, I wish for you to have it, with my heartfelt apologies."

"The older couple that lived here—they are now dead?" Harper nodded. "They were your parents, those monsters? I have no ill will toward you then. I am sorry, but when I felt that it had been unearthed, it was all I could do not to murder the person who had it."

"You can have it, my lady. If it's that important to you, then I want you to have it. I have to tell you, however, I knew nothing about whatever it is being here. Please, take it." Aurora said that she only wanted what was hers. "It is yours, my lady. Again, I'm sorry. And my parents were monsters — the worst kind. And if they stole from you, then all I can tell you is that I had nothing to do with them, and wished them dead for a great many years. Can we be released now? Please?"

"Yes, my child." A word was said and all the faeries stood down. They didn't leave, but they no longer were ready to take them all out. Aurora looked at the black bag, then at Harper again. "You would give it to me freely? Without knowing what treasures are in it?" Harper asked the faerie queen if it was something important to her. "It is. It's important to a great many people and species."

"Then it is nothing that I wish to keep from you. I'm assuming, but I don't know, that my parents took this from you a long time ago. They were killed a few days ago, and we are only just getting around to getting things taken care of." Aurora nodded, then shook her head. "However they came to have it, I'm sorry for it. They weren't nice people, and I'm glad that they're gone. I want you to have that, whatever it is."

"They would be able to lure my people to them. I know not how. I even forbade them to come to this land and the area surrounding it. But they would capture them and tear their wings from their small bodies." Aurora wiped at her cheek, and a diamond dropped to the ground. She looked right at him. "Take it, Samson. I have a plan for you, and such a bauble will serve you well."

He didn't want to. For some reason he had a feeling that whatever it was going to be, he'd end up with a mate as well. Laughing at himself, he picked it up and moaned at the warmth of it, the feelings that it brought to his mind.

Samson looked up at Aurora when she laughed as well, and was granted a wink from her. He knew then that he was in bigger trouble than he'd thought.

"Will you hand it to me, young Harper?" She reached into the drawer and pulled the black velvet bag out. Just as their fingers touched, Samson felt the earth move, and once again he held onto the ground so that he'd not fall back and hit his head. Harper and Bryant were laying on the ground, a soft glow around them. "Harper, you are Bryant's mate. And that is why you will share in the riches of a pure clean heart. This, I have been waiting for since I first touched the little cub that was born on a night with much thunder and lightning. You are, my ambush, the children of my heart, and will have more riches than you ever imagined."

"Wait, wait, wait a minute." Pops got up from the ground and stood in front of the queen. "I don't know about the rest of my boys and Harper, but we don't really need your riches. I mean, it would be nice to be able to help out a few people that need it a great deal, but we don't need for you to make us something we're not."

"And what, my leader, would you think you'd be that you aren't now?" Pops said that he didn't know, but he didn't want it. "You are and always have been a good creature. Not a man, not a cat any longer. You will not allow riches of any kind to make you into something that you are not, Buck Prince. I give this to you for several reasons. But the most important one is that you have never, not once, asked me for anything. You could have. I would have granted you any wish that you asked of me. Money so that you'd not have to go without. Good health so that you'd not get cold in the winter months, or too hot in the summer. And then, when I have nearly given

59

up all hope of finding my lost magic, you returned them to me without a single thought as to what you could have gotten from me."

"Why would I do something like that? Holding something back from you that didn't belong to us in the first place? You do know that Harper is my future daughter-in-law, and doesn't know what you've already done for us. You should be putting the riches where they belong, my lady. I mean, we were put here, and we've been helping in making our kind, the black tiger, a thing of beauty. There wasn't any harm to us in helping out the people around us either. What a thing to say to me after all this time."

Aurora laughed. Her body shone brighter for it, her wings a thing of beauty that made Samson think of jewels and waterways, with just a touch of sun shining down upon them.

"You don't think that I'm having fun with you, do you?"

"No, Buck, never you. But had you asked, at any time, I would have been able to help you all. You should be aware, however, that because you didn't ask, found ways on your own to help yourself and others, your riches are so much more." She looked behind her, then at Harper. "You have suffered more than these men—I know this, my child. You should tell them all of it. Tell them of the things that haunt you still. The stories that would, even though they are men that have been on this earth for more years than anything else, turn their stomach and lighten their hair. Yet, here you stand, giving me what was taken from me without a thought as to what it might be."

"I don't care what it is." Harper blushed. "What I mean is, if I could give back all that was taken from my family I would do it. For you, I'm able to help by returning this item. For that,

I can feel like I've been helpful in some way to my family."

"You are, Harper Wilson Prince, a woman that I will take to my heart too."

Samson watched as the bag was opened. He was as curious as the rest of them as to what it contained. Also, he wondered how the Wilsons had gotten it from the queen. When the four stones were dumped into Aurora's hand—one green, one purple, one a milky white, and a red one—Samson felt the one in his pocket vibrate when they started to rumble in her hand.

The diamond tore from his pocket and landed with the others in Aurora's hand. Another stone, this one of such a brilliant shade of blue that he had to blink several times before he could see again, brightened the others. A sixth stone, this one of the purest shade of green he'd ever seen, settled with the others and rose above Aurora's hand. All of them stood up to look at the beauty of the circling stones in the air around them.

"Bryant, I give you the jade. It will be something that you will need to help you along your path. Please keep it on yourself at all times. Samson, you will have the diamond. It too will help you on your path. And someday you will meet your other half, and she will be more valuable than even it will be. Fisher, the amethyst is for you. You have a rough road ahead of you, but like your brothers, who will be there to help you, you will do well and be happy with your own mate." She looked at Kylan. "I'm glad that you are going to work with your brothers on a new adventure in your life. The ruby will be your shining light in the years to come. And your mate, she will be a shining light that will dull even this ruby I give to you. Harley, you will have the emerald. The color of it will be nothing compared to the beauty that comes to you, with eyes so green that the color of this stone will no longer be bright. Marcus, I wish for you to have the moonstone. It is as rare as the women who will not just own your heart, but they will be the family that you need, and will be cherished by all."

The gems landed on each of their hands. Samson's diamond was brighter than before, and much larger. Samson noticed, too, that the others were larger than they'd been in Auroras hand. He wondered what she had meant about all that she'd said when Aurora stood in front of their dad.

"You've no more gems. But I have to tell you, my lady, I'm glad that you've taken care that my boys are all right now. I am. A father couldn't ask for anything better than to have his children have more than he could give them." Aurora kissed him on the forehead. "Thank you. You've no idea how much pleasure we've all taken in helping you with what you put us here for. It's been a wonderful thing, and we'll continue on with it as well."

"There are no more gems, you are right about that. But I have a better one for you, my dear friend. For all your years of dedication to me, the way you have been unstoppable, no matter the consequences of your life, I give to you two gems, my dear friend." The opal filled his hand, and Aurora smiled when Pops did. "It is, to me, a bit of each of the gems that I have given to your sons. I can never repay any of you for what you have given this earth. Buck Prince, you are a man of men, the real king to my cats, and the greatest man that I have ever known."

"You've given me so much, my lady. I don't know what to say about this." She told him to just say thank you. "I do. I thank you very much. And now that you have your treasures,

I wish to ask you, why did you give them away if they meant so much to you?"

"You all mean so much more." He nodded, and after a touch to each of them, along with a nice hug, Aurora left them with a few of her men to help with whatever they needed. Samson, with the others, wondered what Pop's second gem was.

"It doesn't matter, does it? We have each other, and that's all a man can hope for in this life. Now, let's get this all taken care of." He looked over at Harper. "You tell us what you need and we'll get it."

"I don't suppose you know how to make this land usable, do you? I mean, we will need a home soon. You all are about to bust out of the seams of yours. I figured if we were to use the land the way it was meant to be used, we can all use some of the product from it. For the town." The faeries that had been left behind asked if they could help. "I don't want to impose on you. From what I've heard, you guys have done so much for the family already."

"It will be our pleasure, my lady." They looked at each other, then back at her. "We only ask that you plant us a space of flowers and vinery that we can use for ourselves. That would be more than enough payment for us all."

"You'll have it. In fact, if you give me a list of things that you could use, Bryant and I will be more than happy to supply you with all that you'll need."

They bowed before her, and Samson had a feeling that they were not only going to have a nice plot of land here, but that it would be as bountiful as any ground around.

Chapter 5

Bryant was the first to notice the changes in the house. It was bigger, he thought. Not only that, but he was sure that it had new windows, shutters, as well as a large four car garage around to the left of the house. Pops was the first to comment on it.

"What's going on there? Who is that?" Bryant had been so focused on the house that he'd not noticed the person in the yard. They were looking around as if they were directing the changes. It took him a moment longer than it had his pops to recognize who it was. "Sara?"

Pops took off running, and the rest of them stopped moving altogether. They could only stare at their mother as she hugged Pops. Holy shit balls, it was their mom, back to be with them. Walking with his brothers, he noticed that they too were walking slower. Bryant didn't want whatever was going on to be a joke. His mom was there.

"Hello, sons. I've so missed you." Bryant asked her where she'd been. "We'll talk on that later. Give your mom a big

65

hug, why don't you all?"

They hugged her, each of them stumbling over words and their declarations of love as they stood there. Almost forgetting about Harper, Bryant watched as she stood before his mother and touched her fingers to her hair. Mom let her. It was then that he found his tongue.

"This is my mate, Mom. I'd like for you to meet—"

She cut him off, his mom did, in favor of hugging Harper like she had each of them. It hit him then that Mom knew her, that she'd taken Harper in when she'd needed it most.

"Hello, my dear. I'm so glad that you made it. I so worried for years when I didn't hear anything." Harper told her that her parents were thankfully dead. "Now, normally I'd be upset by such a thing, being thankful that your parents are gone. But to be honest with you child, I'm happy too. They were the worst people I ever met. And your brothers and sister, they're well too?"

"Yes, they're in— You're really here? You're going to be here forever now?" Mom nodded, then hugged Harper again. "I have missed you, Mrs. Prince. Every day, I have thought of you, what you did for me. And the rest of us. You hid food in the fields, and water when it was hot. You also gave us gifts at Christmas and for our birthdays. I never knew how you knew that."

"Oh, well, it's in the county register. That was easy enough. But hiding them, that was a little more tricky." Mom looked at him. "Bryant, I'm so very happy for you both. I've so missed you all. Now then, there is soup on the stove and bread in the oven. And while we eat, I'll tell you what I have been up to. Aurora, she's been keeping me for this day, I think. Come now, lunch is on."

Taking Harper's hand into his, Bryant followed the rest of them into the changing house. He was surprised when no one noticed the new rugs in the living room as they entered, or the furniture that he was sure had never been sat upon. There were flowers, too, throughout the entire house that he could smell. And when they entered the dining room, he was startled to see that not only was the room larger than it had been before, but there were larger windows that looked out on the back yard with a deck and a pool. And right into a large open barn that held not just a new tractor, but also three cows that he could see. He looked around the dining room table, one that he'd never seen before, and spoke.

"Don't you all see this?" Each of them nodded. His mom said for him to just wait. "Wait for what? I'm assuming— The faeries, they did this, didn't they? It was...when Harper said they could help, they did all of this for us."

"They did. Same as they helped me to be able to return. When I was brought down that day, as you well know just my cat remained. But what none of you are aware of is that two of the faeries that were out that day found me there. I was all but dead by then, and they took me, my human self, away." Pops asked if that was why her body was gone and nothing remained but her cat. "Yes. And sadly I can no longer shift then shift back quickly as my beautiful creature, as she sacrificed a bit of herself for me to be able to return one day. You don't mind, do you, family?"

"Are you kidding, love? To have you here again? I wouldn't care one fig if you were a ghost, I'd be just as happy to have you by my side. You have no idea how...well, you might. You might. But I love you, Sara. All the boys do. And now with Harper here? Why, we're a happy family again. No sorrow from any of us." Pops kissed Mom on the mouth, and not one of them teased him about it. "I'm so happy, honey. A happiness that I have no name for, it's that grand."

The soup, thick with meat and vegetables, was delicious as they sat enjoying it. There was hot homemade bread with warm butter to spread over it. And when Bryant was about as full as he could be, the faeries, who had made the meal for them, brought out fresh apple pie with ice cream.

Staggering away from the table, they all headed to the living room to rest. It was then that his family talked about the changes that were occurring in the house even as they sat there. Mom said that it was the faeries that were doing it, but he had a feeling it was more than that. And when one of them came to sit upon Harper's shoulder, Bryant thought they were going to find out a bit about it now.

"We've been awakening the ground since the couple died. The faeries knew that it was going to be turned over to one of the family members, and we wanted to ready it for them. Everything that is here now, it has been just waiting for the day that you were strong enough to take the kingdom of tigers and make them great too. I'm so glad that it is you, Harper. It is a great thing to be working for the one that found the gems." Harper said that she'd done nothing more than to open the safe. "Ah, but you did so much more than that. You gave us hope, a great deal of it. Then when you said that we could help you on the land, all of us wanted to help you in any way that we can. We have started on that for all of you. But mostly, for you and Lord Bryant."

"Lord Bryant?" His brother, Marcus, laughed. "The only thing that he could be considered lord of is his books. And he has a great many of those."

"Nay, Lord Marcus. You are all now marquesses of the black tigers. Each of you has now earned your titles. It is only fitting and proper that you be called lords. As is Lady Harper the marchioness of the black tigers. Your parents are now the duke and duchess of the black tigers. When they step down from their leading role in the lives of all black tigers, then as the oldest born, Lord Bryant will take over as the duke of the black tigers. Each child that you bring into your household to love and protect, they too will have titles. It has, as I said, been a long time in coming."

"But what if we had just dumped the safe and not done anything with it? I mean, it was tempting. I hadn't any idea what my parents might have stored in it." The faerie, his name was Jak, said that they would have figured out a way to guide them there. "You've not guided my siblings to not take this land, have you?"

"Oh no, my lady. We had nothing to do with that. They were not going to take any of it no matter what they had in their own lives. They are settled, the other three. They're happy too, away from here. Nay, they would not have taken it even with the improvements that have been started." Bryant asked what sort of improvements they were working on. "The land, for a start. It hasn't been properly tended in a great many years, even before the Wilsons bought it. We have given the soil richness. Made it into what it should have been long ago."

"You keep saying that. Long ago. Why wasn't anything done to it? I mean, it's a lot of acreage. And for the most part, it's been sitting without a single crop. Why did they, for that matter, plant things this year?" Bryant looked at Jak's smile. "Why do I have the feeling that you all did that as well?"

"We might have had a hand it in, yes." He asked him why. "Because you were able to sell it to the local people, help them along. And even though you had no liking for the couple there, you sold the things with fairness to them and for the others. You're a good man, Lord Bryant."

They asked questions of the little man. When he answered them, each time he would say to the questioner what sort of person they were. A good man. The kind of man that got things started. Or a man that finished things. Helpful, too, was thrown around a lot. It wasn't that Bryant didn't think they were good men, or even kind men, but it was embarrassing to hear it so often. And when two of the female faeries joined them, Jak announced that it was time.

"Time for what?" Mom laughed and told the others to come with them. As they were going out the door, Bryant asked again. "What is it time for, Mom?"

"You'll see. Oh, I do so hope that you love it, boys. It's been my dream since I was awakened in the other world." He asked her about that. "I was told that I couldn't speak of it, and that eventually all the memories of it would fade. But for now, I know what this one thing is about. And as I said, I hope you will all love it."

The walk wasn't that long. They ended up at the property line between his parents' land and Harper's. It took him a moment to figure out what the others were seeing. And when he did, Bryant fell to the ground. A house. Nay, he thought, a mansion.

Jak asked him if he was all right before speaking again. "The other homes will be put around the property as well. Not on this land, but land that we have owned for many decades. The faeries have many people in the offices here in your land that can do many things for us. All the lands that you will each own will not be as large as Lord Bryant's, but they will have a lovely home, one that will hold a family, and have the ability to keep them safe for all time." Harper asked if it was their home, the one they were looking at. "Oh yes, Lady Harper. It is yours. And the rooms, they'll be furnished as soon as the two of you look upon them. The only room that we have taken the liberty of filling is the kitchen. Staff is coming too."

"Staff?" Jak laughed again. Bryant wasn't sure if he wanted to ask him to stop that or to join him. He felt just a little on edge at the moment. "What do you mean, the rooms will be furnished when we look into them?"

The question, like a couple of others he'd asked, went unanswered. As they entered the home, he could see things in it that he hadn't noticed from the outside. There were a great many windows, letting in not just the sunlight, which he loved, but also a view of the yard that was changing even as they moved from room to room.

The first room was the dining room. This dining room table was massive, even compared to the one in his parents' home. There were fourteen chairs down each side. What he'd do to fill such a table was beyond him. A burble of laughter spilled from his lips, and he covered his mouth. Bryant felt like he was on a never ending ride that was going to either kill him or have him committed.

"Will you behave?" He nodded at Harper, then shook his head. "For some reason I can feel your every emotion. Every thought that you have is in my head as well. Behave before they commit us both."

"Are you seeing what I am?" Harper just poked him in

the nose. "What was that for? This is a great deal to take in."

"Yes, so it is. But you acting like a man at the end of his rope isn't helping. Just go with it for now. And once we can sit down, just the two of us, we'll talk about this. But stop trying to figure out if it's real. It is. Shut the fuck up and let me look around before each of the rooms is a padded cell with your name on it."

He didn't think that was very nice, but he knew better than to say anything more. Instead, he did what she said — stopped thinking that it wasn't real and tried his best to enjoy the moment. Christ, they were going to be in the poor house if they had to make payments on all this.

~*~

Mark didn't want to go back to the office. As of right now, the doors were closed up tight and the calls that had come through his office had been rerouted to another center. He hated that he wasn't able to hold onto this one cable outlet. He had others, of course — six that he managed — but none produced like this one did. Or had, if he didn't get Bryant to come back to work. Who would have thought that one man could hold the hearts of so many? Bryant had been well liked, and even loved. Not just by the people that worked with him, but customers as well.

The rest of the employees, about thirty that had survived not being fired in the first place, had found out that he'd fired Bryant and had walked. Just like that — no notice, nothing. If Bryant wasn't there to help them with calls or with troubled lines, then the place was going to fail anyway. He'd not realized that was true until four days after he'd had another one of his cable places send people's calls to this one.

"I have a caller that needs for me to find Bryant. She said

that he always knows what to do to reprogram her remote. The cat stepped on it and messed it up, she said." Mark asked if he'd tried to walk her through it. "Yes. And it's not working. To be honest with you, I think she just wants to talk to him. Where is he?"

Instead of answering him, Mark took the call. After forty minutes of walking her through the steps to reprogram her remote, he finally just handed the phone back to the employee. That wasn't the end of it either.

Caller after caller wanted Bryant to fix whatever it was. Mark might have been suspicious if they'd been all women, but they weren't. There were young men, he thought, from the sound of their voices. Older people that called him sweetie. And one of the calls had even been in a language that Bryant could speak that no one in any of his other centers could speak. Who knew that man was so versatile?

Mark was beginning to realize that everyone had known that but him. Or, and this was more than likely correct, he'd not cared so long as his centers were making an overall amount of money and they didn't bother him too terribly much. But, with Bryant gone and his money maker closed up, he was in serious danger of losing his franchise licenses. And that would end his nice lifestyle.

Picking up the phone, he called the only number he had for the man. When the recording told him that the line had been disconnected, he thought that he might have a way to make the man come back to him. No money to pay even the phone bill might make him a little more receptive to coming back to work. Bryant was playing hardball, that was all.

Picking up his jacket, Mark pulled it on as he made his way to his car. It was brand new, bought before he'd lost

Bryant. Mark was on the verge of losing it and his home too if this didn't pan out for him.

Driving to the house where he knew Bryant lived with his family, he pulled up in front of a house that hadn't been this nice three days ago. Going to the door, he was glad now that he'd dressed in a suit. Impressions, he knew, were the key to getting anything you wanted. Or in this case, what he needed. Ringing the doorbell, he waited for someone to come and answer, and had himself a look around.

Christ, he thought. These people had come into some real cash. Or, he thought, they'd won the lottery. He'd have to look into that part. When the man opened the door and asked him politely what he needed, Mark was certain that he had the wrong house.

"I'm sorry. I thought that Bryant Prince lived here." The man said nothing. "Does he? Live here, I mean?"

"No, sir. He does not." Nothing more, just an answer to his question. Mark tried to think of a way to get answers without begging. "If there is nothing else, sir, then I should like to get back to my work."

"Wait." The man—a butler, he was sure—opened the door wider. Mark had to think quickly, something that he was not at all good at. "Can you tell me where Bryant Prince lives?"

"No, sir. He has a private residence, and as you do not know the address, I cannot give it to you." That sounded a little screwed up to Mark. If he knew the address, why would he need it? "If there is nothing else, as I said, I have work to do."

The door was shut firmly in his face. Mark thought about ringing the bell again, but thought that with his luck, the man would come to the door with a gun.

Sitting on the steps of the porch, Mark tried to think what to do now. Making his way to the place where he'd seen Bryant last, he saw that the burnt out shell of a house was gone, as was the safe that they'd been working on. Looking around the area, he noticed something that he'd not seen the other day—a massive house that looked like one of those southern plantations.

Walking there, he noticed the lushness of the grass—the fields that were planted with what he thought was tomatoes and corn. To the left of those was a well maintained orchard that looked like it was heavy with different sorts of fruit.

Going to the house, he was startled when Bryant asked him what he was doing there. It took his befuddled mind a few seconds to realize that he was actually turned on by the sight of the half-naked man standing there with sweat all over his body.

"I asked you what you were doing here, Mark. I thought I made it perfectly clear that I didn't want to work for you." He asked him if he worked for the people that owned the house. "No, it's mine and my future wife's."

Mark looked at the man, then back at the house. He couldn't help it, he burst out laughing. He didn't know who he was trying to impress with this lie, but Mark wasn't buying it. Instead of believing him, he offered him his job.

"You'll be able to make your own hours if you take it. I can even give you the pay that we agreed on. As you asked before, I can have it put in writing for you." Bryant only walked away from him toward the barn that he'd not noticed before. "There are other perks as well. You can have one of the newest models of cell phones that we now have in our network, with full benefits that you had before. Also, I'll make sure that you have insurance, the best we have."

No answer. But Mark wasn't ready to give up just yet. When Bryant walked back toward the barn, he followed. Bryant was just playing him, waiting for him to give him all of it on a silver platter. Well, Mark hadn't gotten where he was today without having a few tricks up his own sleeve.

The barn was massive. There were several cows in the bins on one side, horses on the other. They were beautiful too. When Bryant went into one of the openings that had a small cow in it, he followed. Mark had never been this close to any animal in his entire life other than a cat, which he hated with a passion.

"Bryant, you do not expect me to give you my job, do you? Come on. You are no more suited to this sort of job than I am flipping burgers." Bryant asked him what he thought he was talking about. "You. Here. You're some sort of farm hand, and we both know that. Don't try and impress me with these lies. I know better. You've always been a man down on his luck, and that is the only reason that you stayed where you are. No man your age works in a cable company helping little old men fix their remote."

"You would think that, wouldn't you? I'm thinking that you've just figured out that not only was I damned good at my job, but I was your top seller. Not to mention, I have been in the number one place for retaining customers for the last six years. Unlike you, I took pride in what I was doing." Mark laughed and asked him if his ego was paying the bills. "I don't worry about money anymore, Mark. I have a good home, a loving family, and a future wife that loves me very much. As for what I'm doing here? I'm enjoying myself. Something that

I bet you never did at the cable company. Other than the fact that it paid for a few toys for you."

"Bryant?" The woman from the other day that had gotten him arrested came into the barn with him. "I just got a job. I was wondering if you'd like to come with me this time. I have to go to some pretty remote place this time, and the company would be nice. What the fuck are you doing here, Mr. Shaw?"

"I'm talking to Bryant. It's a private conversation." She laughed at him. Mark didn't lose his temper. He had a tight control over all his emotions, but this woman just brought out the worst in him. "What the fuck do you think is so funny?"

"You. Do you really think that you can just blow me off with your 'private conversation' shit? Get this through your head, dumbass—he's not going to work for you. You should also know that as of nine-thirty this morning, the board of directors at the company you are working for was informed that you have shut down one of your outlets. I don't know if you're aware of this or not, but you can't just do that without their say so." Mark had known that. It was the reason that he was here today. Before they found out, he'd had hopes that Bryant would get his head out of his ass and come back to work. "Now, I'm going to only tell you this one more time— stay away from my family. And that would include bothering my in-laws. Do you fucking understand me now?"

"So, perhaps it's you I should be talking to. You seem to be the one wearing the pants in his family." He looked over at Bryant and laughed. "My goodness, Bryant. You're letting the little woman here fight all your battles now?"

"Turn around."

He wasn't going to fall for that trick. Mark was smarter than that. But when Bryant said it again, this time putting the pitchfork he had been leaning on deep into the dirt, he didn't seem to have any choice.

There were five of the largest black tigers that—Mark had never seen a tiger before, not even going to the zoo to take a look at them. But he had a feeling that these were larger than even those cats, and they were growling low in their throats. Not that he was sure, but their fur seemed to be standing on end as well.

"Mark, I'd like for you to meet my brothers. I'd give you their names, but I don't think that matters much right now. They're here to make sure that you understand, precisely, what I mean when I tell you that I'm not going to come back and work for you. They're also here to make sure you are well aware of what we mean when we say do not come here again. You understand that now, don't you?" He nodded. "Good. At least we're making progress. When they escort you back to your car, I would caution you to not try to run. Cats, these cats, love to have to chase down their prey before they eat it."

"They're going to eat me?" Mark heard the squeak of his voice, but he didn't have time to worry over that. One of the cats came to stand in front of him and sniffed his hand. Mark was positive that it was going to bite it off. Then he cocked his leg and pissed on him. "What the fuck was that for? This is my—Christ, what are they doing now?"

"Smelling you. Right now it's a little hard for them because—well, you smell like fear. Which is a good thing. We want you to understand that coming back here will get you killed." Mark turned to look at Bryant. He asked him if he was serious. "One thing you might not know about me, Mark, is that when I threaten you, you'd better know that it's gospel. Now, leave here. If you return, you're going to be dead before

78

you can say I'm sorry."

He was indeed escorted to his car. Every few feet he'd stop, just so see if they'd forget him and walk on. If they did, he was going to run. Opening his car door, he looked at them standing there. Mark thought about a million things he wanted to say to them, but really, he was terrified. Getting into his car, he drove off. Christ, this was a nightmare.

Chapter 6

Bryant watched Harper. She was well known in this part of the world, and she seemed to be able to adapt to any situation and speak any language that she needed. When she looked at him and smiled, he couldn't help it—he felt like a teenager in love for the first time.

"They said that they saw the elephants in the lower valley. They've left them alone, but they're worried about them." Bryant asked her what was going on. "There are several calves with them, and the herd is being tracked."

"What is it we can do to help them? I'm willing." She said that she couldn't change things. If she did, then bad things would come back to haunt her. "I don't understand."

"Once when I was in another country, there were several snakes that had been looking for something to hide under in the hottest part of the day. I stupidly made a makeshift area for them, and all it did was cause them to kill each other. You see, it wasn't big enough for all of them, so they fought for the right to rest there. It happens like that all the time. It's why I

81

don't intervene."

He thought on that as they moved along the trail to where the big herd was. Their guide, a kid of about ten, was talking a mile a minute to Harper as he waved his hands. Bryant took the opportunity to look around at the desolate area. His heart was moved by the things that these animals had to endure to survive.

There were few trees that he could see, fewer places of just grass. But there were animals everywhere—some of them atop the trees, others foraging around in the grass for who knew what they'd find to eat. It was a dog eat dog world here, and he would just as soon not be a meal to anything while here.

They stopped for the night and built a fire, which at first Bryant didn't understand. It was hot, so hot that he'd long since taken off his shirt and had wrapped it around his head as a sort of bandana. Then the sun went down.

He couldn't seem to get warm enough, nor could he find a comfortable place on the ground to lie down. Everywhere that he tried to lay his head, he had thoughts of creatures coming to gnaw on his flesh and leave him out there to die.

"You do know that nothing is going to bother us, don't you?" He looked over at Harper. She was making fun of him, he could tell. Asking her why she was so certain, she laughed. "They can smell you. Timba told me the same thing, that we'd sleep well tonight because of the big tiger. It took me a few minutes to figure that out, but when I did, I asked him how he knew. He said that the lady of the land had told him. That he'd be safe enough to leave his mother and brothers at home and help us."

"Aurora?" Harper said that was what she had figured.

"I see. So you let me lay here for half the night waiting for something to come out of the—"

Bryant put his hand over her mouth when she opened it to speak. Reaching to her, he knew with his keen sense of hearing that something was out there. Something that walked on two feet.

Get the young boy and move to the fire. Don't look in my direction. She nodded and touched her fingers to the shoulder of Timba. As soon as he sat up, Harper spoke to him. Bryant moved to the darkness and let his cat take him. He'd worry about what was there when he figured out if they were friendly or not.

They were trying their best to be quiet, he supposed. But to him, they sounded like they were wearing boots that were six sizes too big, and they were breathing hard. As soon as they made their appearance, he knew them to be foes.

"Hello there, little lady." Harper turned to look at them. She cuddled Timba to her, but said nothing. "Seems a little late, don't you think, for a pretty little thing like you to be out here all alone? We was thinking that we'd keep you safe. You know, you scratch my back, I will scratch something of yours, so to speak."

"Fuck off." The men, four of them, thought her funny. He thought that they'd pay for thinking that. And when she stood up, he moved to stand right behind the men. Through this all, Timba kept his eyes on the fire, like he knew just what was going to happen next. "You have any permits for being out here?"

"Permits? We don't need them—we're only taking a walk. Why don't you just sit down, shut up, and let us have some fun? That kid there, he might come in—"

All he did was growl. The men, all armed, turned around and fired well above his head. When one of them cried out, he knew that Harper was trying to protect him, and Bryant leapt at the men, knocking all but two of them to the ground.

Bryant had no idea what was going on behind him. The men weren't moving—he had his mouth on one, his great paw in the chest of the other. The third man was unconscious under him, and Bryant had no intention of allowing him up anytime soon.

"Now, we're going to do this again. Do you have a permit to be out here in the middle of the night? I'm thinking that you don't. Because if you did, you'd know that the rules state several times that you must not take it upon yourself to move around. That something, something much larger than you, will have you for a meal." She laughed. "Pardon my paraphrasing, but you get it."

Are you two all right? Harper said that they were, and asked him if he'd killed the three he was on top of. *Not yet. One of them is out, and the other two might not make it if they don't stop trying to reach for their guns.*

Harper, speaking to who he could only assume was Timba, the kid, came over and took the guns away from the men. He was going on again, and while he didn't understand what he was saying, he had a feeling that the kid was enjoying this a good deal more than he should have been.

A shrill sound nearly had him biting down too hard on the man he had his mouth wrapped around. The men, several of them in uniform, came out of the darkness and gathered the men up. When they left, taking Timba with them, the little boy hugged them both tightly, and Harper spoke quietly to him again.

The exchange was brief. The package that she handed Timba was large, and when he took the little doll that Harper had in her pack, the kid hugged Harper again. Then he turned to Bryant. He lay on the ground, his big cat still taller than the boy was.

"He wants me to translate for you." Bryant told Harper that was all right with him. "He said to tell you that he is going to tell his village that a great black tiger saved him tonight. That he and the lady had stopped the poachers from taking their friends."

Tell him that it was my pleasure to have been a service to his friends. I'm assuming that he means the elephants here. She said it was every living creature. *Tell him that I'll stop by the village on our way out with payment for watching over you for me.*

When he was told that, Timba hugged him again. After licking his skin to make sure that he knew Timba's scent, they parted ways. As soon as he could no longer hear the men and Timba, he shifted back to himself and stood before Harper naked. Bryant was as hard as stone.

"As much as I'd like to take you up on the idea that we could fuck around out here, we can't. When I said that we were protected out here, I meant because the police were nearby." He nodded. "You're not mad at me, are you?"

"Good heavens no. Why would you even think that? I have the rest of my life with you. We can, as you put it so sweetly, fuck around anytime that we want. I do have a request, however. When we do return home—alive, right? —I want you to teach me some of the languages that you speak. Just enough to not get me killed when we're doing this."

They laid down together after Bryant pulled on a pair of shorts. After shifting he was warmer. The fire was bright with warmth and light, and he found himself falling asleep almost as soon as Harper curled around him.

Waking up to Harper nudging him in the chest, she told him to keep his mouth shut. Rude, he thought, then he sat up. Christ, they were all around them — elephants of every imaginable size — walking around them, crushing the packs that they'd brought in. Harper was taking pictures. When she stood up, he was a bit nervous until he realized they didn't care what she was doing, he supposed, so long as she was moving slowly to do it.

"When you stand up, make sure that you keep your head down at first, just to show them you mean them no harm." Bryant did that. And when the small elephant, the calf, came up to nudge him with his trunk, Bryant reached out slowly to touch his fingers to his large floppy ears.

He'd thought it would be stiff, or at least somewhat hard, but it wasn't. His ear was as soft as his own flesh. Bryant knew that Harper had been sent here to take pictures of the herd, but what he'd not expected was to be so up close and personal with them.

"That one is about four months old." Bryant asked how she could tell. "He's enjoying what little grass he can find. But he still won't stray far from his mom. I think he likes you, Bryant."

They stayed for most of the morning. Bryant was careful to not get knocked down by the big beasts, but more importantly not to get in Harper's way. She was changing the next canister of film when he realized that he'd not taken a single picture to send to his family.

"I have some that I can share with them. Christ, that was wonderful. And seeing them through your eyes was about the best thing that I've ever done. Thank you for coming with me." He asked her if she was finished. "Not yet. I need to get a few more shots in to finish off this roll, and I thought that we'd see if we can track them for a while. Just because we can."

They were about two miles down the road when they came across the herd again, but the scene was far from beautiful this time. They'd been hunted and found. Bryant felt his cat and his rage come over him in huge waves as he looked down at the dead baby calf that he'd just enjoyed the morning with.

The only satisfaction that he got from it was that one of the men had been crushed to death, and a second one looked as if he'd been gouged with a tusk. Their guns, too, had been broken. The biggest of the elephants, the bull, seemed to be mourning the loss.

Three of the elephants had been killed, two for their tusks. The mother of the calf had also been murdered, and lay partly in the water that they'd been heading to, Bryant supposed. Her young calf lay dead beside her with a gunshot to the head. Bryant asked Harper if she knew why they'd killed the baby.

"He would have been crying when she fell. It may only be an animal, but he'd know that his mother was gone. The others in the herd would have tried to protect him, but I'm betting that he'd not have wanted to leave her side." She put her camera away after taking some more photos. "The male will lead them away tonight. Today he'll protect the dead as best he can from other animals. We should get a move on. The smell of blood will bring out a lot of beasts."

Bryant wanted to stay and bury the dead, but that would be nearly impossible to do for a single man. He also knew that there was an order to things, and that if he did that, then he'd be depriving other animals of something to eat. The circle, he knew, needed to go on.

~*~

The flight back wasn't too bad, but she longed for a hot shower and a bed. Harper hadn't ever had one of these shoots upset her so badly. She wanted to blame it on the men that had murdered a family they'd played with, but that wasn't it entirely. Harper had seen the day through the eyes of another — the animals being what they were; friendly, curious animals that hadn't done anything to anyone but have valuable tusks.

"I was thinking about something." She nodded and asked Bryant what it was. "These pictures that you take. Do you sell them all to the place that hires you? Or do you have a stash of them like the ones that you took today?"

"A stash. A huge stash of them. I'll take upwards of three hundred or more pictures when I go out on these things. Then, if I'm in a good mood, I let them look through them all and decide which ones they want. Most photographers take a lot, but they have digital. I prefer using regular film." Bryant asked her why. "Two reasons. One is that I love to look at them, sometimes enlarge a few of them. Second, it's harder to steal someone's work when it's not on a computer or out on the cloud. Not that I'm completely untrusting of those things, but I started out with this sort of camera and have stuck with it. I have my original camera too."

"What if you made a book? Just put where the location might be on the cover, and then let the person looking at them decide if they want to learn more about the happenings that are going on. I don't know how much detail you'd have after so long on some of the pictures, but me, I'd just leave them with the pictures." She asked him why again. "The money could go for a way for the animals to be protected. I know that they're being very proactive about dyeing the tusks of these beautiful creatures so they're not valuable to poachers, but that has to cost money too. We, or you, could help that cause by, I don't know, donating the proceeds from the sale of the books."

"That's brilliant." She knew she'd been loud and lowered her voice. "I love that idea. And your brother, Marcus. He could put them together, the good and the bad, in an order that would appeal to most everyone. Christ, Bryant, that's wonderful."

She knew people who knew people, she told him. Also, Harper had a couple of people that owed her favors that she could tap to help with the advertising. Actors and actresses that would see the value in doing this and help out. Bryant took notes, as he did on most things he was starting out, while she scatter gunned things at him. He was glad to have been able to take her mind off the last shoot.

By the time they landed, he had a list for her. He had also talked to Marcus, who was as excited as Harper had been when he'd brought it up. They were well on their way to getting something together at their home when his parents pulled up. With them was her brother, Randy. The man did not look all that happy.

"I need you to come to my hotel room with me." Harper asked if the kids were all right. "Yes, just fine. I need for you to see Tyler and Meggie. Right now, Harper."

The house was finished, but Randy didn't seem to notice. Whatever was on his mind, it was blocking out the fact that not only were they living in a new house, but that it was huge too. It would hit him later; Bryant would bet that then he'd feel embarrassed, and more than likely not mention it at all.

Bryant decided that he was going with them even if he was told no. Telling his parents that he'd meet them at their house later, they said that they'd take their bags and equipment into the house. Dad told him to call if there was anything they could do.

The ride over to the hotel was made in silence on Randy's part. Bryant could tell that Harper was getting more and more pissed as they rode there, because her brother wouldn't tell her anything.

Tyler was sitting outside in an old rocking chair, just swaying back and forth as if he had not a care in the world. Harper called his name, and when he looked at her, he had the biggest grin on his face. Whatever was going on, it seemed to be only upsetting Randy.

"Hello, sis. How the hell are you? If you're wondering about me, I can tell you that I've never been better in all my life." This was perhaps the oddest thing he'd ever been a part of. When Tyler asked her to have a seat next to him in the other rocker, Harper did so without hesitation. "I've been out and about, looking at the town from a new perspective this morning. Randy, as you can tell, is having a cow. But then he's always been the worrier of all of us."

"What the fucking hell are you talking about?" Bryant would have laughed, but he knew, even if her brothers didn't, that she was about as pissed as he'd ever seen her. She looked at Randy. "I thought for sure that one of you was hurt. That you'd fallen down the stairs or something. You rushed me back here to find out that Tyler has been looking around the town? Why? You had better have a good reason for this,

Randy. I've been in a plane for over fourteen hours, and I need a shower, a meal, and sex. Not necessarily in that order, but if you fuck with any of them, there will be hell to pay."

When Meggie came out of the hotel room and joined them on the porch, he could see that she'd been either up for a long time or she'd been drinking. He wasn't sure that she did drink, but who knew with this group today? She was dancing around, singing, and looked like she'd just grabbed whatever she could touch to put on. Stripes and polka dots did not go well together.

When she handed a sheet of paper to Harper, Tyler laughed again. They were all intoxicated, and that was why Randy wanted Harper? It didn't seem like that big of a deal to him. He'd never been drunk himself, but he wasn't human. Then Bryant started listening to what was being said instead of how it was being spoken.

"I can write my name. See that? I can write my name as clear as a bell." Harper started to hand it back to her sister, like him, thinking that there was something wrong with the lot of them. "Look at me, Harp. Just look at me."

It took him too long to figure out what she was showing them by waving her hands, *both* hands, at them. When Tyler stood up, just like he'd done it every day of his life, Meggie started to squeal with happiness. Watching Harper, he didn't think she was taking it as well as the other two were. When Harper looked over at him, he could almost feel her disbelief.

"She said to me that I could heal mountains with a touch. That I could heal anyone that I loved with just a thought. Just before Aurora left us, she told me that. And that my family would be whole if I were only to enjoy the love that Bryant and I have together." Bryant asked her when she'd told her that. "It was to me—in my head. I think that when I touched her to give her the bag, we formed a connection. Like you and I have. But this one is odd. I can see things too."

"So, this mysterious woman tells you that they're going to be whole again, and you figure that is why Tyler is no longer in a chair and Maggie just had her hand appear? For Christ's sake, Harper, what the fuck are you smoking?" Before he could figure out her intent, Harper slapped Randy. "What the hell was that for?"

"Think, you fucking moron. Think about what you just said. They're whole. And I bet you are as well." Bryant didn't know what she was talking about, but Randy cupped his cock and shook his head. "You've been using other men's seed for all this time to have a child. I bet that you can father your own children now. As many as you wish."

"They said that the damage was too bad. That I'd never be able to have it reversed." All Harper did was take Meggie's hand in hers and slap him in the face with it. Several times. "All right, you've made your point. Fuck, Harp. Do you really think so?"

"I don't know why not. When they told us that Tyler would never walk again, something about the vertebra never holding up or something, we took that as gospel because we knew nothing about the safe, the magic stones, or what I would get from it." Randy cocked his head at Harper. "Never mind, it's all making sense in my head. Even with Meggie's hand. They told us that when it had been cut, thankfully with a hot blade, that they couldn't reattach it because of the way it had been cut. Burnt off at each end."

Bryant was going to have to talk to Harper. He wanted to talk to all of them, to find out what had happened to them.

But he wasn't sure how they'd take talking to a near stranger. Randy looked over at him just then and nodded.

"We have to bring him up to date on all of this, Harper. I know that they're dead, but we all still have nightmares about what they did to us. We could never talk about it before, not fully, because of the threat hanging over our heads from them." Randy looked at him. "How about I buy us an early lunch and go someplace and have a long talk?"

"My parents, they'll want to know as well. They were a part of this long before we knew anything about the four of you." Randy looked at Tyler and Meggie, and when they nodded, so did Harper. Randy told him to bring in all the family, if he didn't mind. "No. But can I ask you a favor, Randy, all of you? I'd like for you to consider moving back here. They're gone. The house, believe it or not, is nearly finished. I'll explain that as well. I know that Harper would love for you to be here, to be able to stay close to you, and I'd very much love to get to know you all."

"I'll think about it." Meggie said that if Tyler would agree, she would come here to live. She felt alive again. "I have a very pregnant wife at home, and two children. We'd have to talk about it, the four of us."

"All right. I'll get in touch with my family and we'll meet after lunch. You're not going to believe the fun we had on this shoot, Randy. Someday, you should go with your sister. She's really good. I've grown to have a great deal of respect for photography after that trip." Bryant shook Randy's hand. "Together we can do this, Randy. I know that you have an aunt that has been notified, and with us being away, we've not heard what she is planning to do. But if she pulls anything, any shit on you at all, she's going to have to deal with the

Prince family. Which, I might add, includes all of you."

They walked to the little pizza place around the corner from the hotel. Tyler was in such a wonderful mood that it rubbed off on Randy and the rest of them. Before they left, Bryant was able to contact his family and made a time for supper. They were all going to be there. It was then that Bryant realized that they'd be eating in the new house for the first time as a group. He wondered what changes had been made to the big house that he'd grown up in, and knew that he was going to miss the old place. It did have a great many fond and amazing memories for the Prince family.

When they arrived at the house, Harper asked if she could take a nap. When she woke, she told him, they'd talk too. He could tell that she wanted to go and get the pictures started. He wondered briefly if she did the developing herself or sent them out. Bryant had a feeling that not only did they have a darkroom if she needed it, but it would be well supplied. Going to the bedroom with her, it wasn't until he laid down beside her that Bryant realized how exhausted he was too. In minutes Harper was sound asleep. He wasn't far behind her.

Chapter 7

Michelle hung up the phone after making arrangements to go to the little town in Ohio. She wasn't sure how she felt about her brother being dead, or that nasty person he had been married to. According to the attorney that had called, it was just discovered that Margaret had killed Randal and then set fire to herself. Why? No one seemed to have an answer for that. Good riddance to them, as far as she was concerned.

The children would be adults now, all of them devastated in some way about their parents. Not their deaths—Michelle knew they'd be happy about that—but about what they'd done to them. The things, unspeakable things, that had been done to them that she, at one time, had been all right with. Then she'd gone to see Tyler.

He'd only been a little boy. It had taken some time for her to remember how old he was. But when she saw him lying there, strapped up to every machine that the hospital had to keep him alive, realization had hit her. And it hit her very hard.

"Do you know how he was hurt, Michelle Wilson?"

Michelle looked up at the woman there. She didn't know her, not at all, but she still seemed to be someone that she should know. Michelle had shook her head, and the woman seemed to float towards her to have a seat.

The chair that the woman sat in hadn't been there — Michelle knew it. But there she sat in a larger chair than the one that she was in. Days later, trying her best to remember what her face had looked like, all she could remember was the glow that seemed to be surrounding her.

"They were driving home from the grocery store. No food for the children, who were nearly starved and in need of a good bath. No, they'd bought themselves steaks and large potatoes. Would you like to see what happened next?" She didn't answer her, of that she was sure. But the delight that Michelle had felt that her brother had taken control of his children had been there too. Also, a bit of sorrow for the fact that they were so hungry. But the touch, a single finger to her heart, changed everything in her life that day.

Tyler had been in the middle of the back seat. Randy had been holding onto Harper behind Randal, who had been driving. Michelle thought that Harper should have been buckled in as well. Meggie was by the door.

Tyler had to pee — he was sweating with the need. Michelle didn't know how she knew that; perhaps it was the way he was holding himself. The other children were watching him, hoping, she supposed, for their father to pull over for him to go.

"You have to pee, did you say?" There was a tone there — Satanic, she thought. And when they pulled over, Margaret got out of the front seat, climbed into the back, and unbuckled the boy. Michelle was confused when Randal started the car back up and took off down the road. With the door opened, Michelle was afraid that one of the children would fall out. Then it happened.

Margaret jerked the little boy out of the seat and tossed him out of the fast moving car. She watched as he bounced twice, his little head bleeding as he went through the air the second time. And when he landed on the side of the road, his back hitting the curb hard, she knew that whatever she had thought had happened to the boy was a lie — her brother had told her that he'd fallen from a tree — and that the other children had suffered equal horrors.

The film, or whatever she was watching, drew back to the car. The three children were still sitting in their seats. Their father could be heard laughing hard, only second to the sound of Margaret's laughter.

"He fell from a tree, you hear me?" All three nodded, Meggie crying so hard that she could hardly catch her breath. "You shut the fuck up, you little cunt."

The slap — not the first one, she knew, to Harper's face — bloodied not just her lip, but her mouth as well. Why she touched the child was not known to her, since it had been Meggie that was crying. But as they sat there, for God knew what reason, she hit Harper again and again until she lost consciousness.

Michelle looked at the woman when things stopped.

"There is more. More of the same. Sometimes it is worse, other times so bad that they wish for death. They will ruin Meggie's life with their ways. Harper will become cold, distant but for her work. Tyler will never walk again, never have a life outside the four walls that he keeps himself in.

Randy will not know the joy of having his own child. He will rely on others to make that happen for him and his wife to be."

"Can I change this? Can I save them?" The woman shook her head. "Then why do you torment me with this? Why do you show me these things if they are to come to pass, and I will be helpless when they need me?"

"They know you only as a monster like their parents. They will not contact you. Nor will you ever know of their lives, the love that they have inside of them. The way that they help each other through the bad times and good." Michelle asked if there would be good times. "If things are not changed for them, then no, they will never know anything but suffering. But I think they'll escape from them, go away to be as safe as they can make themselves."

"Tell me what to do. I'll do anything. I knew that my brother was...I had no idea that he was like this. This horrific. I need to help them." She told her that she couldn't, not yet. "When? After Margaret throws them from another car? Perhaps this time in front of a truck? No, you need to tell me what I can do to help these poor children."

"There will be a time when someone will tell you that the parents are dead. Much damage will be done to each of them before that point. But you'll come to them then." Michelle was nodding. "They might not ever trust you, Michelle Wilson. You will have to not just open your heart for them, but to listen and let them get to know you. The woman that you can be."

She had ended up back at her home. To this day, Michelle didn't know how she'd gotten from the hospital to the airport, much less home, where she'd been when it occurred to her that she had to make changes in her own life to be able to be what the children would need of her. And she had.

Sitting at her little desk, Michelle thought of all the times her brother had called her, telling her one lie after the other. How Meggie had lost her hand in an accident. He'd never been clear on that, what she'd done to do something so horrible. But it had only taken her a few phone calls to find out what they'd done to her.

Harper had done something. Michelle's private detective never could find an answer to that question, but they were going to make her suffer, to make her pay for her crimes. According to her resources, there were many "crimes" that Harper committed. Nothing, however, was nearly horrible enough for the child to pay the way that she had.

Margaret had made Meggie hold onto her hand, hold it there so that they could burn her. When she refused, apparently, Harper had told her to go ahead, to burn her, she didn't care. Her defiance was legendary, Michelle had heard. It had been what Randal complained about most.

But Meggie was made to hold her wrist, her detective had learned. Harper had assured her that it would be all right, that she'd be fine after it was over. Then when the ax, white hot from the flames that they'd put it in, came down, it not only cauterized Meggie's hand from her wrist, but made it so that attaching it again wouldn't work.

Harper had been beaten then. She had launched herself at her mother, and had nearly killed her, it was said. The only thing that it had gotten Harper was six days without food or water, in a well that had been drained many decades ago.

And now, Michelle had been informed of their parents' death. Her butler came into the room with a cup of tea and several cookies on a tray. Setting them in front of her, he sat on the arm of the couch and asked her if she was all right.

"I am now." He asked her if they were dead. "They are. I shall need to pack, and book a flight. And those photos, I can't forget those either."

Michelle looked over the fireplace at the picture that hung there—one that Harper had taken. One of her first, actually. She'd taken it long ago, just after Michelle had made sure that the camera fell into her hands.

"I have the mind to go with you." Which meant that she was going to be traveling with her friend and sometimes lover, James Star. When she nodded, he went to the kitchen to start plans.

They'd made these plans years ago. It had taken him and the rest of the staff a bit to get her on the right path to change the way she'd been before, and it depressed her to know what sort of person she had been. But it had worked—more than worked. Michelle had changed her life so much that the children of the town no longer feared her, but would come by when they were selling things just to sit with her for a while. And the parties that she had in the summer for the families of the burg that she lived in were legendary.

No one was harmed. There was no blood shed, unless someone fell, and there certainly wasn't anyone that walked away hungry. Michelle also held fundraisers, helped with local charities, and supported the schools as if her own children, of which she had none, would go there to learn.

In two hours they were ready to go. The staff would have the month off. Michelle figured that it would take at least that long for her to get her family to trust her. The food had gone home with the staff too. She had no animals to care for. No matter how much she tried to have herself a dog or a cat, she just could not make herself like it. So, unlike a lot of older people, she didn't have an ankle biter. The other fallback that she had from her former life.

"We have a room at the local bed and breakfast. The children are staying in the hotel, and I thought it best not to let them know that you were there." She asked if he knew whether they still owned the hotel. "You do. While I was talking to the woman at the desk, she told me that Harper has attached herself to the Prince family."

"Attached, or has she married?" James told her that was all he could get out of the woman without raising suspicion. "Yes, I can see that. They're a good family. A little down on their luck, but someone that I would have chosen for her as well. And the others? They're all right now?"

"As far as I know. The young lady said that she'd seen Tyler walking around yesterday — she must have been mistaken — but she said that all the Wilson children are back, and that they're so sweet. Unlike the parents." Michelle nodded, nervous now that they were seated on the plane. "You'll be happy to know that the house has been demolished, or what was left of it, and they're building. There were no services for the parents."

"Good. And the will, it's not changed at all has it, that you know of?" James told her that he didn't know that part. "Well, I can only assume that it hasn't. And the children, they know nothing of my part in their lives, I'm hoping. Nor the others."

"No. They'll know, of course, once you get there. It's only right that they find out what you've done." Michelle wasn't so sure. She was nearly sixty-nine years old, and she was afraid that the children, grown adults, would hate her once they saw her. "You're worrying overly much, Michelle. Just wait until they get to know you, and you'll see. They'll love you as much as, if not more than, I do."

"You love me because I sleep with you." He burst out laughing, and several people turned to stare at them. At another time in her life, she would have stood up and berated them, but she only sat there, laying her head on James's shoulder. "I have to make them understand, James. They're all I've lived for all these years."

The flight wasn't long—too short, if someone were to ask her. All these years of prepping and planning came down to this one meeting. And then after that, she'd either be going back home with her tail between her legs, or she'd have a family again. One that she hoped would take her to their hearts.

~*~

Harper was at the airport when the plane landed. She knew who was on the plane—she had spies everywhere. It had paid off well over the years to have someone on her payroll, and now—well, now she was terrified that this one woman was going to tear everything in her new little world apart.

Aunt Michelle came through the doors with an elderly man at her elbow. It took her mind a few seconds to realize that they were in love. Also, the woman that she'd come to hate with all her breath was smiling. When they both walked by her, Harper sat down on the chair next to her, thankful that it was where she needed it.

"Well? Was she on that plane?" She nodded at Bryant. "I see. And you're going to just sit here rather than talk to her. I

102

thought we talked about this."

"You talked and expected me to listen to you." Harper looked at her. "Why today? Why is she here at all, Bryant? She was told that there was nothing in the will for her. She's just coming here to what, take up where our parents left off?"

"I doubt that at seventy, she'd have that much energy." Harper corrected him. "All right, sixty-nine then. Not that it makes a hell of a lot of difference. She's older than you. You, my dear, are in great shape. I know that first hand."

"Behave, will you? Men and sex." Bryant pointed out to her that she'd been the one that had jumped on him last night. "So? It's not like you fought me off that hard. But back to my aunt. What does she want?"

"Would you like to ask me that?" Harper stood up and looked at her aunt. She hated to admit it, but she looked fantastic. "I thought it was you standing here, but it's been so long. Harper, honey, thankfully you don't look like either of your parents."

"What does that mean?" Bryant cleared his throat, reminding her, no doubt, that she was supposed to wait before throwing out insults and punches. "I don't want you here. I've heard enough about you to know that you're no different than they were. Perhaps worse."

"You have the right to think that. I've given none of you, not even my brother, any reason to not think those things." She looked around, and so did Harper. "I don't suppose you could introduce me to your young man, and I'll do the same with mine. Then perhaps we can get something to eat. I've been very nervous about coming here, and I just realized that I'm hungry."

Helping gather up their luggage, no one said much. The

cases were beautiful, something that she might have picked out for herself. There was also a great deal of it. Before she could stop herself, Harper told her aunt that she wasn't going to be staying with her.

She'd hurt her aunt—the pain flashed over her face so quickly that had she not been looking, Harper would have missed it. When Aunt Michelle walked away, she started to follow her, but James asked for Harper to give her a moment. No, she thought, she did not want to give her a minute, and went after her.

"I'm sorry." Aunt Michelle nodded. "No, I'm really sorry. I'm not usually this— Well, that's not true, I'm forever rude. But to you, that was uncalled for. You may stay with us if you want."

"I have reservations at the bed and breakfast." Her aunt stared at her. "How did you do it, Harper? How on earth did you survive them? I know what they did to you. All of it, I think. What I don't understand is how they didn't break you."

"I'm stronger than they were, I guess." Aunt Michelle shook her head and told her that it was more than that. "I don't know. I guess long ago I decided that I was going to be better than all of you."

"Yes, I can understand why you'd lump me in with them. But I'm not. I was, for a very long time, like them. Or so I thought. Then I went to see young Tyler." The men came up behind them then with all the luggage. "We're staying at the local B&B, so we'll just head—"

"No, you'll stay with us." She realized that she'd been harsh. "Please? We'd like—I'd like for you to stay at our home. We have plenty of room."

She didn't think that her aunt was going to give in, but

after several long seconds she nodded and said it was all right with her, but that she'd have to have a car. Bryant explained to them both that there was an extra car at the house if they wanted to just use that.

There wasn't a car there, at least not an extra one. Neither of them had decided on what they wanted while talking about it last night until after they'd gone up to bed. Then when they'd gotten up this morning, not only were the cars they'd decided on in the garage, but they were loaded with everything that could be had on a car, as well as the colors they wanted. Harper, like Bryant, figured that since they'd decided on them, the faeries had gotten them for them. It would be the same for the extra car as well, she'd bet.

Aunt Michelle didn't talk much on the way to the house. James did—he asked about the others. It was on the tip of her tongue to tell him it was none of his business when Bryant squeezed her hand. She didn't know what was wrong with her. She wanted to punch the woman in the face one minute, then do her deathly harm the next. There was no in-between for her right now, and as soon as they were home, Harper made her way to the dark room that had been put in.

~*~

"This has been hard on her." Michelle said that she understood. Harper had taken off the moment they'd pulled into the driveway, and hadn't looked back. Bryant wasn't mad at her, but he was embarrassed for the other couple. Michelle asked if they should go to the B&B. "No. I don't know why, but I'd have a feeling that she'd go get you, and you might be safer if you don't let her do that."

He'd meant it as a joke, he really had. But like everything he said when he was nervous, Bryant fell short of the mark.

After showing them to the room they'd have, he also showed them around the house. They were sitting on the back deck with a glass of tea when Michelle finally spoke.

"I'm not being rude here, Bryant, but I had heard that you didn't have money. I know that Harper does, but this—this house looks like you've lived here forever." Bryant told her she wasn't rude, but it felt like that to him as well. "It's none of my business, is it?"

"No, but I'll tell you. I don't mind. When I met Harper, she was here for the death of her parents. To make sure they were dead, she told me." Michelle said she could understand that. "Yes, well, I met her out at the garage. She told me what they'd done to her. I'm sure there is a great deal that she's not saying yet, but we have a long time together."

"I've changed from the person that Harper and the others knew." Bryant wasn't sure who she'd been before, but he sort of liked whoever she was now. "I came here once, when Tyler was hurt—they'd broken his back. A beautiful woman came to see me. I never can remember her face, and if she told me her name that day, I don't remember it. But she showed me a great deal that day. You'll think me off my noodle, but all she did was touch my heart and there it all was. The children were hungry and dirty—beaten too. I saw that too, how Harper was beaten by Margaret. She also told me that things would never be good for them, not if I didn't change my ways."

"You've been helping them, haven't you?" Michelle told him he was smart. "No, just observant. I don't know in what ways you might have been there for them when they left the house, but I'm sure that you didn't allow them to fail, or even to be hurt again."

"No, I tried. But there were things that were simply out of

my control. To be honest with you, Bryant, the only help that I was able to give your Harper was to see that the camera was there for her to get. After that, she did all that on her own." Bryant knew that of Harper. Even behind the lines, she'd be wary of who she got help from. "I wished every day since that day that I'd been able to help them more. To somehow put things that they needed there for them. But I was told, by the woman, that I had to wait. That my turn, if I would only change, would come to me. It's why I'm here."

"I'm going to be honest with you, Michelle. I don't know how much luck you're going to have with any of them. They're hard and bitter. The only one...well, lately that's not true of Meggie and Tyler, but Randy is a broken man. I think he's just waiting all the time for something to befall him. His wife is coming here soon. They're thinking of moving here—all of them are. But it's going to take a great deal more than a few moves to have them trust you." Michelle nodded, and then James got up to leave them. "I'm sorry. Did I upset him?"

"Oh no. He and I—well, we're more than just employee to employer. James has been my rock and teacher since this happened. He was there when I was failing—and I did at the beginning. And he was my teacher to show me how to be what I wanted all along—a gentle woman that didn't harm those that she was supposed to love." Michelle looked in the direction that Harper had taken. "I was going to take the children when my brother died. They would have had a better life, but not much better. I would have taken them to task—beaten them too, I think. But I don't want to think that I'd have starved them, or locked them away for days at a time. But I honestly don't know what I would have done before Tyler was nearly killed. And Harper hates me."

107

"She's all hard crust on the outside, but she's hurting too. In ways that I can't touch." She asked if she still had nightmares. "Yes. Before we found out you were coming here, we'd planned on meeting with the family to talk about everything. Some things that I'm sure are going to hurt us because we didn't help them in some way when they were children. But if they all don't talk about it, then at some point, I believe it's going to hurt them more than my family."

"Your mother." He nodded. "I didn't find out until much later that she was doing things for the kids. I know that when the children were in that well—oh my, that well—but when they were in there, I found that your mother had dropped them down food. Did you know that it was mostly Harper that was punished for things?"

"Yes. I'm sure that you'll get to talk to Harper, but what one thing can I tell her that would make it so that she'd talk to you? There has to be something. Not that I think she'll trust any more than she does now. But it's hard to tell." Michelle pulled her purse—pocket book, she called it—to her and pulled out a thick notebook that was tattered and worn in places. "You want her to have this." Bryant took it, but he wasn't sure if this was a good idea.

"I do. There are things in there that might make it so that she at least understands what I was doing by not stepping in when I wanted to so badly." Not sure what he should do, Bryant didn't pull the dark blue ribbon off the notebook when he took it from the elderly woman. "If you could hand her that, I'd very much appreciate it, young man."

When she stood up, so did Bryant. He was torn, if he was honest, but he'd do it. Michelle said that she was going to have a lie down, and that if they didn't mind, she'd love to hear what was said at his family's house. But she didn't need to come to dinner.

"If you show up at my house and then tell my mother that I hadn't invited you to her house and insisted that you stay to eat, even as old as I am, she'll beat my butt. You'll see that my mom, Sara, is as mean and stern as she is loving and kind. And every one of her boys are terrified of her."

She was still laughing when she headed back into the house. Bryant let his family know what was going on, and told them again about the talk. However, the longer he sat there thinking about the book in his hand, the more he regretted asking Michelle for something to give Harper.

In the end, he went to find his mate, and hoped that he'd be able to have dinner with his family and wouldn't be dead in the ditch someplace between here and his parents' home. Smiling, hoping he was right and that Harper couldn't kill him, he went to the dark room.

Chapter 8

Harper wasn't mad — well, not really. She was upset, but that wasn't as bad as it could have been. She looked over at the book that Aunt Michelle had wanted her to read. So far all she'd done was to take the ribbon off. Harper looked at Fisher when he cleared his throat. She'd not even known he was in the library with her when she'd entered.

"I thought you should know that it's not a blue ribbon. I mean, it is blue, but it's not just— It's blood stained." She picked up the ribbon, wondering how he knew that. "I can smell it. I'm sure that Bryant could too when he gave it to you, but he was too nervous to notice. He didn't want you to be upset."

"I'm not sure what I feel right now." He nodded and asked her if she trusted him. "I do. All of you. I just don't know my feelings toward my aunt at the moment."

"If you let me touch the ribbon, I can find out about it. I'm sure in some way it has something to do with you and your sister and brothers." She asked him what he could get from it.

111

"Other than smell, I can find lost things. Sometimes, if there is a great deal of emotion attached to the object, I can see things that happened to it. In this case, I'm assuming that with the blood, there is a horrific story that goes with it."

She thought about what he said. Horrific. Her life up until she left home had been that daily. Now she was as happy as she'd ever been. Plus, just this morning, she'd figured out that she was in love with Bryant. A new and amazing feeling for her.

"I started to ask you why you thought it would be horrific, then I remembered who I am. Not that you completely understand that, but to offer something like this to me, you have to know that it's not something nice." Fisher said that he knew that too. "I don't want you to be hurt with whatever is on it. I don't mean just physically. I mean at all."

"I thank you for that, Harper, but the memories from it won't hurt me, but they will hurt you." She nodded. Then she asked him how she was to give it to him. "Just hand it to me. If it is indeed your memory, you've already touched it at some point. Are you ready for this?"

"No. But my aunt wanted me to have this. And I have a feeling that the only way I'm going to open this book is if I know all of it, don't you?" He nodded. "May I ask you a question, Fisher?"

"Absolutely. But be warned, my dear sister, that I will forever tell you the truth. Even if I didn't have to, I would." She asked him where he'd gotten his name. At his burst of laughter, Harper figured that she'd caught him off guard. "Fisher. When we were first made into humans, we were just babies. When we got older, Pops told us to pick out our names, and to think hard about it. Until then, I'd just been called Three. Like the rest, in the order we were born. I think we all shifted on the same day. That's it, it was on our tenth birthday. The field we did it in wasn't far from where we are now. There was a creek there at one time, that— Never mind. I get on rolls. As cats, tigers, we knew nothing of being a human. How they fed themselves, lived in homes. Much less learning to walk and talk like they did. Anyway, we were learning how to fish. This was a few hundred years later, of course.

"We were watching the man across from us in the creek fishing for a treat that we'd never had before. To watch the beautiful way the man used his pole, the string flipping in and out of the water, was poetry to me. The back and forth motion was soothing to me, having just shifted from beast to human after running down my meal. As I watched him, not knowing that fly fishing was an art, I realized that it wasn't just the fact that the man was more than likely feeding his family, but he was also relaxing. Taking his time to enjoy what he was doing in order to provide for them. And it was then, after being called Spot because of the single spot on the back of my head, that I decided that was what I wanted to be—a fisher. The name stuck."

"What a lovely story. I don't suppose Bryant's is that romantic, is it?" Fisher said that she would have to ask him. It was, actually, a funny story. "All right. I'll let you do this for me, but know that whatever it tells you, you have to tell me everything, okay?"

"Yes. I'd have it no other way, love." He took the ribbon from her. Harper knew that it was stiff in places, and she'd just assumed that it was just old. But now that she knew what was making it feel that way, she almost didn't want to do it. When he locked eyes with her, she knew that Fisher was getting more than he'd bargained for. "The blood is yours and Tyler's. You wrapped it around his finger when he was eight to make sure that he didn't bleed to death. What you didn't know, and he never told you, was that he was bleeding more from his back. That the cut on his finger was nothing like the beating that he'd just received by Margaret using a whip on his back."

"This was before he was thrown from the car." Fisher nodded. "I wasn't very old either. But he came into the house and collapsed. He would only show me his hand. It had a splinter in it as deep as the bone. I know now that it was from gripping the pole he'd been chained to."

"You thought that if you tied it off, his finger, then you could take the splinter out without giving him too much more pain." Harper nodded. "He wished for death. Did you know that?"

"Yes. I think daily that we all did. Wanted to die to end the misery that we were in. If we weren't being beaten nearly to death, then we'd be starved. My parents would make us sit at the table with them while they ate a huge meal with meat and vegetables." She thought about the day and the ribbon. "Bear with me, Fisher. I'm popping in an out of stories to deal with them, all right?" Fisher nodded again. "I wasn't allowed to feel pretty. The ribbon, from a trash heap behind the house, was there one day, and Meggie took it for me. I was only able to wear it when we were alone. Tyler had been chained to the pole the day before. I had snuck out there around midnight to take him water and a cracker. It was all I'd been allowed to have, if I remember correctly. When he came in the house that next afternoon, I think I knew that he was hurting more than on his finger, but I could only deal with—as I am now, I suppose—one thing at a time. When he passed out, I was able to roll him over and...and.... She had beaten him so badly, Fisher, that his ribs were showing. Not that he had any fat on his body anyway, but they were nicked with the whip she'd used. I despaired of him surviving, and like him, wished in a small way that he wouldn't. We were all so abused."

"What had he done?" Harper stood up and looked at her aunt, who was standing behind her with tears rolling down her face. "What had he done, Harper, that would have her do such a thing to him?"

"He was hungry. We all were hungry all the time. He only wanted to know if he could have another quarter slice of bread." Aunt Michelle asked if that was all they'd had to eat. "Us kids, yes. Margaret and Randal had red meat or other meats for every meal, if I remember."

The hug was consuming to her. The arms around her, soft and firm, had Harper stiffen from them. But when she heard her aunt sobbing, the sound of it like a breaking heart, she found herself wanting to comfort her. To give her something that Harper hadn't had, something that none of them had had as children.

Hugging her back seemed like the right thing to do, but only for her aunt's sake. Then, as they held onto each other, gripping hard on whatever they could clutch, it became clear to her that they both were getting a great deal from the touching of souls. That was what it was—they were touching each other's souls and giving them comfort.

"I had no idea. Not until so much later." Harper told her aunt it was all right. "No, it's not all right. That woman, she told me that I would abuse you as well if I had come to get you then. And she was more than likely right. But I've changed so much. Not toward your father. I promise you, whatever he told you I was telling him, it was all lies so that I could bring you home with me. I wanted him to believe that I was just like him, a sadist. A person—nay, child, he wasn't even human as far as I'm thinking, but he was a monster. And to let me continue to hold out hope that I'd be able to bring you all to my home, as you were already in my heart, I had to pretend."

"What woman?" The room seemed to have brightened a great deal in those seconds. Turning around, she noticed that Fisher was gone and that Aurora was standing in the room. "Aurora, did you tell my aunt not to come for us?"

"I did." She looked around the room and smiled. The warmth of it seemed to touch every part of her. "Come, the family has assembled. Let us go and talk to them. I believe that Tyler has very good news for you as well."

Harper didn't want to go and sit with the family. She wanted answers, and wanted them right now. But Aurora took her aunt's hand and they left her in the room alone. The notebook was lying on the table where it had been, the ribbon there as well. Picking them both up, she clumsily dropped the papers that were inside of it.

They were newspaper clippings, old ones, some of them. Tattered too, in ways that made her think they'd been looked at over and over. She picked the one on top up and read about her first magazine contract, how she'd won a prize for taking a picture of salmon leaping in the air at Yellowstone National Park.

There were others too, about her brothers and sister. Meggie had become a renowned painter, despite being one handed. It went on to tell that she'd lost her hand in an accident long ago, and how Meggie had said she'd learned to adapt. Tyler invented games for children, teaching about abuse and what to do about it. Randy had made many millions of dollars, and the article told what he did what a great portion of it. He, like her and the others, donated it to the homeless and abused children.

Picking it all up with shaking hands, she made her way to the living room. She staggered twice, her mind reeling about not just what she'd read, but the fact that her aunt had bothered to collect them. She'd not read the notebook as yet, but she had a feeling that it would be an eye opener. Not just for her, but the rest of them as well.

As soon as she entered the room, she could tell that they'd been fighting. Tyler was standing up, his body stiff with anger, and was shouting at Aunt Michelle. Randy was moving toward the door, to leave she'd bet. Meggie was sitting on the floor, as if her legs had just given out on her. The Princes were trying to get everyone to calm down, to no avail.

Harper put her fingers in her mouth and let out the loudest whistle that she'd ever been able to produce. Looking at Sara, Harper apologized before speaking.

"Sit the fuck down and shut up before I shut you up. Mother fuck, this is not the way that I wanted you guys to sit down and have a talk. And if you leave, Randy Wilson, I will hunt you down and beat your ass. I'd not fuck with me right now, I'm just in the mood to do it." He put his arms over his chest, and she looked at Bryant before looking at her oldest brother again. "I will have Bryant shift and knock you to the floor if you don't get your fucking ass over here and sit down on the chair."

When Randy looked as if he wasn't going to stay, Bryant

117

stood up, along with the rest of his brothers. Sitting down, Harper could tell that Randy was pissed off, but right now, she wanted answers more than she was willing to try and coddle her brother. Telling Tyler to sit too, he said that he'd been sitting most of his life, he wanted to stand.

"You can stand so long as you get that fucking rod out of your ass and relax. This is for the Prince family, not for you all to get your asses puckered up like someone is going to fuck you in the ass." Sara cleared her throat and Harper looked at her. "I did tell you I was sorry. But sometimes you have to get fucking pissed before people start to pay attention to the bigger cat in the room. Now, we're going to calmly and quietly talk about this. And if one of you gets out of hand, I swear to Christ, you'll think that I've turned into a she-devil, and I will hurt you."

"She said that she's been watching over us and did nothing to help us." Harper told Tyler that she had done a great deal. As she went through the newspaper clippings, Tyler continued. "Well, fuck that shit. Why didn't she help us when we were with them?"

"I wasn't in any position to help you then. Saying that I was just like your parents isn't quite right. I had no idea what they were doing to you children. We—Randal and I— were 'disciplined' when we were children—severely so. But nothing like they were doing to you children. So, like a fool, I went along with it, telling him that should I have children or were to have you children, I would treat them the same way he was. I swear to you, I had no idea that all the times you were getting hurt were not accidents." Aunt Michelle looked at Aurora. "She came to see me when I was notified that you were in the hospital, Tyler. I had no idea how you'd been hurt, only what Randal had told me. That you'd been climbing a tree and had fallen from it. All the stories that he told me about you being hurt, I later found out, were untrue. She showed me what had happened that day, and she told me that if I didn't change my own ways, if I didn't become someone else, other than the person I had been, then you would die before you were old enough to leave home."

"You could have helped us at some point. Did you know that we all lived on the street until we could figure life out with real people?" Aunt Michelle said that she did. Harper handed Randy one of the many articles about how he'd won a great deal of money and had purchased a house. "You did this?"

"Yes. A great many other things, too. I knew that you'd never allow me to come into your lives. That you'd never trust me if I just showed up, not that I blamed you. So I pushed things around so that you were getting help from me without you knowing. Tyler had a good wheelchair so that he could move himself around. Meggie had paints and canvas when I discovered what a wonderful talent she had. The first camera that Harper got, I made sure that she got it. It was my father's, you see. I took it to hock when I was younger, and had forgotten about it until then." She looked at Randy. "You won the money because I made it happen for you. I made sure that the winning ticket for the money, money that I put there, had your name on it. You didn't even try to win, but you had to. Don't you see? I did help you. Anytime that I could."

"I didn't know." Aunt Michelle said that was the point. "I know, but when I think back on things— You did more than that for us all, too, didn't you?"

"Yes. But it will never be enough. Not ever. You children,

119

you were forever in my heart. Forever on my mind, and I could not love you more if you were from my own body. You mean the world to me." Harper handed out the rest of the clippings so that they could read them. "I kept up with your lives as best I could. When I could. Finally I had to have someone watching over you every day. The only one I had trouble with was Harper. Finally, I just had to give up and hope that I could help if she needed it. Now, I don't know about you all, but I'm starved. Tyler, you sit next to me, please. I need to know how it is you can walk. Then I'd like to talk to Meggie. It's a miracle, I have to tell you. A wonderful miracle."

~*~

Bryant looked at the photographs that were hanging to dry. He knew that Harper had been taking pictures while he'd been playing with the elephants, but he'd not realized how she'd caught him in a lot of the shots. She was putting up a few more when she finally spoke to him.

"I won't sell the ones with you in them. I mean, usually, I just let them pick out what they want. But those mean a great deal to me." She pointed to the one where he was leaning over the dead calf and mother. He'd been crying at the waste of it all. "Except for that one. I couldn't have asked for a better display of emotions than you have there. I'm betting that he asks for more with you in it. The others show your face and that one doesn't, so he won't know who it is. He'll just be able to see the powerful passion of a person, and that is what I'm going for. I'm not willing to share you with the world, Bryant. But this man, he'll only get that one if he's nice to me."

"Why do you like this one?" The calf was nudging him on his legs, and he could almost feel the joy again. Both their faces, the calf's and his, were a study in happiness at the treat

120

of seeing each other. "Harper?" He turned around to look at her — she was staring at one of the pictures.

"I have them. Their faces. I know who the people are that killed the herd."

He went to stand by her, and it took him a moment to figure out that he had no idea what she was looking at. Then after she pointed them out, he could see the five faces from the brush, looking right into the camera. "The police there, they'll know just who they are, and will be able to bring them in. The money they're making off of killing elephants is high. This will help them catch them, so that at least a few other herds might make it."

He didn't know what she had to do, but he would help her as best he could.

After hanging the picture to dry, she checked all her baths, the shallow tubs that she had been using to develop the pictures. Then she opened the door to make a phone call. It took her nearly thirty minutes to find someone that could help her.

"Yes, I can send you a print of the picture." She paused. "No, I'm afraid that won't fly. No one takes my negatives. Those are mine."

He looked at the other pictures. Knowing what to look for, he found two more pictures with the faces on them. Then he found one that had something more in it. Taking it down, careful of the print, he showed it to her when she paused in her conversation. Harper immediately closed the connection.

"Well, fuckity fuck. The cops there are in on it. Now who do I call? I'm guessing that's why he really wanted the negative." Bryant asked if she'd given him her name. "No. I don't even use my correct name when I'm applying for permits. The magazines that I work for, they're required to make sure I have the proper paperwork."

"I might know someone you can call."

She nodded, and told him to take care of that and she'd get this done. Harper enjoyed this part of what she was doing. Not that he blamed her. Just watching her do the work, he was intrigued with the way the process worked. Bryant decided that he wanted to learn how to do it so that he could help her.

Mark was at the front door when he came out of the dark room. James, who had been helping out with the training of a butler, was talking to Mark. And when the door slammed in the younger man's face, James turned to him.

"He has a real hard on for you to come work for him again." Bryant laughed. Such a prim and proper man saying things like that really tickled him somehow. "What can I help you with, Lord Bryant?"

"First, stop calling me that." He looked over at Timothy, the new butler, and Bryant gave in. "All right, but just try not to say it too much. It sort of gives me the willies or something. I'm going to have Aurora come here in a bit. She so loves your cherry scones. Do you think it would take much for you to whip her up some? I have a favor to ask of her."

"There are some coming out of the oven now, as a matter of fact. Also, she left me some of her special tea blend, and I'll have a nice pot of that ready for her as well. Go ahead, Lord Bryant, give her a call, and we'll be waiting for her." Bryant asked if the deck was finished yet. "Yes, I heard this morning that all they were waiting on was the bulb team. They're planting bulbs in the planters there so that they'll come up all the time. I didn't ask to come by and see to the pots. Sometimes— I don't know about you, but I find it easier

122

to just let it go. Don't you?"

"Yes. Yes, I do. Like just this morning. I got in the shower, and when I turned off the water and reached for the towel, the entire room was flipped around. The colors were all different, and we had a linen closet in there. I just nodded and went on." They were both laughing as he went to the yard to call out to Aurora.

The yard was so green it hurt a little. The flowers in the planters around the front porch were in full bloom, and long tendrils of vines were hanging down almost to the dirt. Like at his parents' home, there was a brick sidewalk up to the front of the house with tiny flowers, rather than dirt or sand, between each block. He loved the outdoors, and having his home sitting here, beautifully ready for any kind of entertainment, or even to just sit out and hear the animals in the late evening, was something he was very proud of.

Closing his eyes, Bryant thought of the lovely queen. She had been around a great deal more in the last days, talking with Harper and the other Wilson children. She was also helping Harper with the magic that she'd received. He had as well, but he was already used to having it, so it didn't freak him out as much as it seemed to freak out Harper.

"I'd not tell her that, if I were you." He smiled at Aurora, and told her that he had no death wish and wouldn't do that. "She's a lovely girl, your mate. Are you happy, Bryant?"

"I never thought I'd be this happy." Aurora sat on one of the rockers, and he sat with her. "Harper takes pictures in the wild — you knew that, didn't you?"

"I did. We are excited to see the book when it comes out. She will have to sign me a copy so that we can all enjoy it more. Now, what can I do for you, my dear cat?"

Bryant explained to her what they'd figured out. Showing her the picture, it was easy for her to see the exact location where the picture was taken as well. But since she wasn't able to interfere with human issues, she could, she told him, get help for them.

"He will be most cross with me for telling him to come here. But then again, he's been idle these last few months, so perhaps he might enjoy being around your family. I certainly do. You remember Jack Winhall, don't you?"

"The former vice-president? I do. He's been doing a lot of work with the environment and global warming. I've not seen him in years." She said that she had, only just last week. "Is he still aging himself? I've never seen a person so obsessed with making himself look older."

"He has been playing with other things with his magic as well. One of them is the preservation of a couple of species that are nearly gone. I will give him a call. See what he can do to help you and your family." She disappeared, then returned with a man nearly as old looking as a corpse. "I think he's gone too far. Do help him, Bryant. Perhaps he just needs to meet a woman. That would certainly make him sit up and behave himself."

"I don't need a damned woman, Aurora. Having you bothering me is quite enough, thank you very much." Jack looked at him. "If you're going to look like this all the time, Bryant, perhaps I can take some lessons from you. Damn, but you're a fine looking man."

"Thanks. I think. And so you know, I'm spoken for." They both laughed at that, and Jack joined them on the deck. When a table and four glasses appeared filled with lemonade, he figured that they were about to have company. "I have a mate. She's doing some work with some of your projects, I guess."

"I know her. Beautiful young woman. You're her mate? Neither of you could do any better, I don't think." Harper came out of the house with a handful of pictures, as well as a notebook. Not at all like the dozen or so they'd gotten from the safe. "Harper Wilson, how the fuck are you?"

"Jack? Christ, did your chair finally break under all that bullshit that you have? I've never seen a bigger blowhard than you are." They hugged tightly, and Bryant laughed when another rocker appeared. And almost as soon as it was there, it was replaced with a regular chair. He'd forgotten that Harper didn't care to rock. "What brings you here? Dinner isn't for a few more hours."

"You have never had respect for your elders, young lady." She snorted, and Jack laughed. "The lady queen here tells me you have some information for me. I'll take care that it gets taken care of, child. You can bet on that."

"The police are acting as guides for these poachers. And sometimes, from what I gathered from my sources, they take the tusks while the bull is still living. Sick bunch of mother fuckers, if you ask me." Harper handed him the picture as she told him about the phone call she'd made. "I'm thinking that sooner rather than later, something is going to blow, and there is going to be a major system crash there. We need to act now."

"I'd say that you're right. But then, you usually are. All right. Give me about an hour. When I get it taken care of, I would like very much for you to wait on selling these pictures." Bryant asked Jack what he meant. "She's going to have to give these pictures, the one of the poachers, to the newspaper. I can take care of that for her. I have to say this, however; you do know this is going to make you a bit less popular for a little while."

"I don't care right now." Harper looked at him. "I'm seriously thinking about opening a shop in town. Taking some kiddy pictures with their dogs and have some off time. This being on call all the time, it's for the birds."

"Good for you. Also, I'll make sure that you don't get any credit for this find, all right? I know how you work the system when it comes to having people know who you are. That should help out a bit." Jack looked at him. "A long time ago, you told me that you were going to save everything that you got in order to sell it when you were old like me. Do you still have that crap?"

"The furniture and other things? You know me, Jack. I never toss anything that I might still be able to use. Why do you ask?" He told him. "I don't know, Jack. Why would someone want to put it in their home? I mean, I can see one or two pieces, but all of it?"

"I'll have some people that I trust go through it with you. Some of it, by now, might be worth some cash. Not that you need it now, but there is never a time when you should turn it down."

Jack left with Aurora a few minutes later, after taking time to see the barn that they'd put things in over the years.

"Are you all right?" She nodded, then shook her head. "Anything I can do to help you out, honey? You look exhausted. Not only that, I don't think you've been sleeping all that well either."

"No. I would very much like to sit down with this cash we have here and divide it up." Bryant said that was fine with him. "Good. I'm going to talk to my family again, see if they're going to object to having some of this. If so, I want to divide it equally between your brothers, parents, and my aunt. She might object too, but I have a feeling that she's planning to move here, and I'd like for her to be able to take that cruise that she's been talking about."

"She must have said something to Pops and Mom. They've been talking about it as well. Mom is having a good time putting up the things from our combined gardens. And the fruit." Harper said she'd had some of his mom's apple cranberry jam. "That is by far my favorite thing of all time. She also makes this relish with zucchini and green tomatoes that will knock your socks off when you put it on a hot dog."

Bryant went into the house with Harper. Almost as soon as she sat down on the couch, she was asleep. Covering her up with a soft blanket, he went to make a few phone calls. There was something he could do for Harper, and it was going to make her smile.

Chapter 9

Mark straightened his tie again. He was nervous, as nervous as he'd ever been. Being called before the franchise firm that owned the rights to his cable company was something he'd not planned on doing today. Well, any day, as a matter of fact.

The call had come at six-thirty last night. There was no telling them to fuck off; the woman on the phone had told him, not asked, that he was to be at the meeting at eight-thirty sharp, and to bring his last two financial records. He was to also bring his employee roster. He'd not been sure what that was, but when the email came with all the items he was to bring, there was an explanation of everything.

Thinking about the last paperwork he'd gathered of his financial records, he'd not realized that not only the cable company that Bryant had worked at showed that he was the best at his job, but apparently he'd been holding up all his companies. Out of the six that were still open, he figured that Bryant was making about half of all his sales. And that was saying a lot, as he had about three hundred people that were supposed to be working for him. He'd take care of that number, to make sure they understood he was in this to make money, as soon as he was done here.

"Mr. Shaw, the directors will see you now."

He knew this was the woman that had talked to him last evening. She had a voice that would make a person shiver like nails running down a chalkboard. But this wasn't the time to get pissy with anyone. Thanking her politely, he entered the room.

"Mark, I've been doing a bit of research on your businesses with my name on them. What the fuck have you been doing?" No, "Have a seat, would you like a drink?" Just both barrels hitting him as soon as the door closed behind him. "Sit down and hand over the paperwork. And for your sake, do not try and fill in the silences with chatter. I cannot stand a person trying to save their job by excuses when it's probably too late."

Too late? What the fuck did that mean, too late? He'd done just what they said, Mark and had even been twenty minutes early. The paperwork was all there. Why call him in here if there wasn't a snowball's chance in hell of saving his job?

The woman that entered the room a few minutes later, he knew. It was the bitch who had gotten him arrested when he'd been trying to talk Bryant into coming back to work for him. And then Bryant entered the room.

If he'd not noticed the woman, he might not have known Bryant. He had on an expensive suit and tie. His hair, usually unruly and dark, was pulled back behind his neck in a neat ponytail. It perfectly suited the man, as well as making him seem years younger.

Clearing his throat just to make sure they knew he recognized them, Bryant spoke.

"Hello, Mark. You'll be happy to know that my wife

and I have bought out the controlling interest, as well as your contract for your call centers. In addition to that, we've also called in an auditor to make sure that we're not buying something that is already out of reach to bring back up to par." He asked him what the fuck he was talking about. "I don't know how to explain it to you any other way. You're more than likely going to be terminated, I would imagine. Also, with you losing your job, we've decided that you're going to have to move out of the house you're in. From what I was able to figure out on my own, you've been charging your payments to the company, and since they've made more than half the house payments for it, we've taken possession of it."

"You can't do that." He looked at the other people in the room. "He can't, can he? I mean, he worked for me. Sucked up all the overtime when it was there. Won contests that he always traded in for cash. Christ, this is a joke, right?"

"I'm afraid it's not. I've known Harper here for a great many years. She took my daughter's wedding pictures for me. And every year since, she's been there for us to take a family portrait. She's not one to mess with, young man. And it seems that you have shit in her oatmeal by harassing her husband. You really screwed up with this family." Mark didn't remember the man's name, and since no one else had introduced themselves, he was at a loss as to what to call any of them. "You should have been a better boss, Mark. I'm sure that you're figuring out what I already knew. Bryant Prince is about the best there is at talking to people. Because of that ability, he's become somewhat of a closer, if you know what I mean."

The man stood up, and in seconds, it seemed to him, Mark and Bryant were the only two in the room. Bryant had loosened his tie and pulled off his jacket. When he'd done that, Mark couldn't have said. He had been too busy wallowing in his own misery.

"How could you do this? I don't mean to me, we'll get to that. But how the fuck could you have gathered up enough money for you to have been able to buy me out? Did you start dealing drugs or some shit?" Bryant only laughed. "Seriously, what the hell did you do to me?"

"I did nothing to you, Mark. You fucked up your own life all by yourself. As Mr. Augustus told you, you should have been a better employer, as well as man. You aren't, I'm just figuring out. Did you really think that you could get away with charging your lifestyle to the company to claim that it wasn't making a profit?" Mark told him it had been working until he had to get a burr up his ass. "So this, your failure as a businessman, it's my fault too. I see. Well, I guess, as the saying goes, it sucks to be you."

"You can't fire me, Bryant. I mean, how will I live? I've no other job that I can do that well." Bryant pointed out that stealing from the company was not a job skill. "Shows how much you know. I was good at it. No one caught me in all the years that I've done it."

"Regardless, you're not going to be able to return to your lifestyle at my call centers. I've put a guard at each one of the places we now own. Your badge, as of the moment that the call was made to you last night, has been disabled. In addition to your home being taken from you, so have your company credit cards. The bank accounts that you have, all of them, have been sealed, and you're not to touch the money until such time as you pay back what you owe." Mark again asked him how he was supposed to live. "Frankly, I don't care.

You were willing to and did fire me when I told you that my family needed the money to make ends meet. Now that I have a little more leeway in things, I can see that not only were you a bastard about a great many things, but you have also been cutting payroll down to cover your losses at the tracks."

"I love gambling. So what if I lost a few hundred bucks?" Bryant corrected him. "There is no way that I owe a quarter of a million dollars. You have that wrong."

A sheet of paper was pushed toward him. It had all the days he had been at the tracks in the last year, as well as how much he'd bet and lost. It was only for the last year, and he'd lost that much. He couldn't fathom how much he'd lost over the last fifteen years of gambling. Pushing the paper back to Bryant, he said that it proved nothing.

"Perhaps not with just your lousy gambling habit, but when you put it all together, it does prove a great deal. Mostly that you aren't cut out— Let's just say it…you're not a very decent human being." Mark just stared at Bryant. He'd never heard him say a terrible thing about anyone. "I just never had the opportunity to be able to not care what I say to people, so long as it's the truth."

Mark left after turning in his keys to everything that he thought he owned, as well as his badge. They all knew that it didn't work, so why they needed it was beyond him. Going out to the parking garage, he looked for his car where he'd parked it, and realized that they'd not wasted any time. Taking his car from him meant that he had no way of getting home, wherever that might be from now on.

Mark knew that he had about six hundred dollars on him. It was, he supposed, all the money he had in the world at the moment. While he was contemplating the cheapest place he could go get something to eat, he realized that he was no longer going to be able to cash in his retirement fund either. He wished right then that he'd thought about putting money in an account that they'd not be able to find. Christ, he was such a dumbass.

The police were at his home when he got there. There was a bag on the front porch that he'd never seen before, and when the cop standing there saw him, he brought the bag to him. It was heavy, and his thinking that it might have money in it was short lived when Officer Bonner spoke.

"Bryant said we were to find you something to wear around. He also gave you some cash so that you'd not starve between jobs. I don't know who would hire you after this hits the paper, but there you have it." Paper. He'd not thought about how this was going to be public. His mom was going to have a cow. But then, she'd always told him that he'd never amount to anything. "Also, Mr. Shaw, there is a court ordered hearing on your behalf in ten days. I'm going to hand the subpoena to you now. I have on a body camera, so you will be recorded when taking it from me."

"Yes, all right."

It wasn't this guy's fault that he'd fucked up. So signing the form and taking the paperwork, he didn't even bother reading it. Putting it in the duffel bag, Mark was resigned to the fact that he was so fucked right now, he'd be lucky if he could enter a grocery store and not get arrested.

Mark used to run four miles every day—he'd loved being in shape. Today, the walk from the meeting to the house had worn him out so much that he felt as if he needed a nap. Right now, on top of everything else, he thought that taking a nap on the road where he could be run over sounded like a wonderful idea.

Moving toward a hotel that was outside of town, he passed a pizza joint. They were hiring. There was an added note on the sign that no experience was necessary, but would be helpful. He'd eaten pizza before. How hard could it be? Slap a little cheese on some bread, or whatever it was called, and voila, it was finished. Going inside, the scents and the hunger he was feeling seemed to have tripled in that moment. After going to the counter, a burly man asked him if he had an order.

Explaining that he was there for the job, the man looked him over like he was sizing him up. Asking him questions as he answered two questions from the back, the man told him that he'd need better shoes, shorts, and that he'd supply him with one meal a shift, all the drinks he wanted, and what the pay was. Minimum wage was a far cry from what he'd been making before, but he took the job. Christ, how far had he fallen, he thought as he sat at one of the tables with a bottle of pop, the man called it, to fill out the necessary paperwork.

After he was finished, he felt like a fool. Mark had taken the first job that he'd come across, and was making pizzas and subs for a living. He was going to have to find himself something better. This was not a job for him. It was a job for teenagers — No, a job for Bryant.

Going to the hotel an hour after getting a briefing on making pizzas, Marks mind was a mess in trying to remember all the shit there was to do. Christ, had he been wrong about slapping them together. They were more complicated than matching his suit and tie with a decent silk shirt. Now all he needed was a car to find himself a good pair of shoes. He wondered how much that would cost him, as well as a pair of shorts. He'd not owned any shorts that were black since he'd gotten out of choir practice as a kid.

Getting a room for the week was by far cheaper than one by the day. He hadn't any idea what he was going to do about furniture once he found a house to buy or rent, so the hotel was going to have to do for now. This way, he told himself, he'd have clean sheets every day, as well as fresh towels.

Mark thought about getting back at Bryant, but he knew that was a pipe dream. The man had five of the biggest brothers he'd ever seen—not to mention, they were tigers. Who would have known that? Certainly not him. There was also a thought about turning him in. But what sort of fool would he look like if that didn't pan out? Yeah, he could see the headlines now; Former Boss Tries to Say His Employee is a Tiger. That would go over as well as him stealing from his company.

~*~

Kylan looked over the spec sheet he'd been given earlier today by his boss. Ace had to be a fake name, Kylan thought. But his boss, Ace Miller, had left it for him to do. It was for a not for profit coat drive. While he could understand charging people ten bucks to get in the door, the little note at the bottom of the specs said that there would be a charge of ten dollars for each coat, hats would be two for ten, and gloves would be marked with a price. Kylan looked at the cubicles around him and wondered who he could ask about such a thing.

He thought of his mom. After telling her what he was doing, she tisked about it.

People are donating the coats, you say? He told her that they had donations of all kinds of things, but the drive was advertising the coats for this one. *And that's all donated as well. What do you think is going on, Kylan? You're a smart boy. You know as well as I that something is up.*

Yes, I thought so as well. But after having my boss go over everything on this thing with me, he took off for lunch. He and I are supposed to be working on this together. He usually runs off on something he has going on until I finish the work up on my own. Mom asked him why he was still working there. *I like the job. Also, I think I'm pretty good at it. There have been other things like this that come across my desk, all not for profits that have some sort of prices attached to them.*

Is it always the same company? He pulled up his own spreadsheet, the one that he used to take notes on each of the pitches that he took care of. Kylan told Mom that it looked like it was. *Then I'd say that you're right in questioning this. I don't know what sort of trouble you could get in for doing that and it not being true, but the simple fact that in your heart you know that it's wrong worries me greatly.*

This is something else, Mom. I'm to make sure that on the final copy of this, the firm's name is nowhere on it. It has said that on the last several of them that I've done — no name of the company, like they're hiding it from the public or something. Mom asked if his name was on it. *I haven't ever signed my work with a signature. I have a code number, different for each of my pieces of work that I tag them with. It's always in the same place, but the codes are always different.*

Kylan would put the four digits of the spec form he'd been given from his boss. If he didn't use an actual form, like all the not for profits were, Kylan would scan it to the spreadsheet that he had made up and attach it that way. The number that he gave it would be in the notes. After the last drawing was approved by his boss, Kylan would send it to the painting department to be filled in. He'd then attach a photo of the completed work to his notes before going on to another job.

What is the name of the not for profit, son? I still have some contacts that I can call on to figure this out for us. Like you, I thought that not for profit meant just that — no one was making any kind of profit. Now, if the company was going out and buying the coats, then that would be a different can of worms altogether. Kylan laughed with his mom. He was so glad that she was back. Today had brought home just how much he'd missed her. *Let me ask around. I don't know just yet who it is I'll ask, but I'll get back to you on this.*

Kylan worked on the advertising for the rest of the day. He had several more days in which to finish the work, but he never liked to leave something for the last minute. While he was buried deeply in what he was doing, he was startled to look up for a moment and see Randy there. He asked him what was going on.

"I thought we had a lunch date. You did say one, didn't you?" He looked at the calendar on his desk, then back at Randy. "Come on, I think it's my turn to pay. I have a couple of ideas about what you and I were talking about just yesterday. And my wife arrived with our children today. I don't know who arranged that, but I surely do appreciate it."

Kylan, even though he was fuddled a little, did the same thing he did every time he walked away from his computer. He put all his files away, saving them on the thumb drive that was his own. Closing the tabs he'd had opened for reference on things, he pulled the drive out and put it into his pocket. As the computer was being turned off completely, he was glad now that he'd changed his password that morning. Kylan had also saved the paperwork that Ace had given him on the new project, the way he usually did.

When they were out on the sidewalk, Kylan still having no idea what was going on, Randy told him that his mom had called him. Nodding, still sort of clueless, they walked to the deli that Kylan had been wanting to try but hadn't, because he'd forget and work through lunch. Which happened to be the only time they were open.

After ordering, they found a seat in the back of the place and sipped their drinks. It wasn't until Randy showed him pictures of his children taken in the hotel that he smiled at him. Kylan looked around when he nodded to his left.

"There is your boss. I didn't know what he looked like until I was in here yesterday. He's a bastard, did you know that?" Kylan said that he didn't know if he was that devious or not. "He is. When I first started out making a few bucks here and there, I decided that I needed someone that I could trust with my money. The same was going on with my other siblings, making money and not having a great deal of trust. So, while it might have taken me a little longer than most, I became an attorney. For us. But, I do have an international license simply because I do a lot of long distance traveling to make some of the profits that I have. That is why when your mom called the hotel asking if I might know an attorney for you, I jumped at the chance to help."

"You mean because you feel like you owe us something." Randy told him that was some of it. "I'm sure you've been told, but we don't feel as if you owe any of us anything. We're just glad that it's turned out so well for Bryant and the rest of us."

"It has, but for us too. Having Aunt Michelle around, talking about us like we're real human beings, people that she is very proud of, it was more than we ever expected coming here. I'm sure you realized that the only reason we did come here was to make sure that our parents were dead."

"I understand that as well. I cannot even imagine what you all must have gone through growing up with them. Nor that anyone checked up on the four of you." Randy changed the subject by asking about his job. "Normally I just do the design aspect for the things I'm working with. But with these projects, I do it all, from concept to finished product. The only thing I don't do is color them in and print them. I know that this is an odd thing to do, donations not for profit. And I don't think I would have been so concerned if not for the fact that I'm beginning to not trust my boss. You might think he's a bastard, but so far, nothing has been untoward to me."

"Yesterday while I was sitting a mere three feet from him and two of his drinking buddies, I overheard him talking about how he had you on the end of his hook. I wasn't sure what had brought that up, but when I say I overheard it, I mean, anyone in the place would have overheard it as well." Not really wanting to know what he had to say, Kylan asked Randy about it. "You're a sap, did you know that? And he can get you to do anything illegal that he wants by just laying it on your desk. He told his two drinking buddies that you're doing work for him that will never see any kind of worksheet, as it too is illegal. The only person that he knows will get into trouble for it is you. Since, and this is a direct quote, you're too stupid to—"

When Randy picked up his glass and started drinking, Kylan had a feeling that his boss was coming toward them. Instead of waiting for him to get to the table, Kylan stood up and faced the man. Not only was it Ace, but his two buddies too. Just as he opened his mouth to tell him off, he saw Officer

Bonner, acting police chief, sitting behind Ace, watching the two of them.

"Did you really think that I'm so stupid that I'd not cover my ass when it came to doing what you told me to do?" Ace looked around. Kylan could see by the look on his face that he'd not expected him to figure it out. "The not for profit flyers that you told me to do. Do the people that donated the coats know that you're going to be charging people for them? As you did the turkeys at Thanksgiving last year. Or worse yet, you charged each family sixty dollars per child to receive, again, donated items."

"I don't know what you're talking about. We didn't charge anyone. The only thing that I can think is, Prince, is that you put that on there yourself. Why would you add that at the bottom of your work if you're not making any kind of money from this?" He pointed out that if he didn't know about it, how did he know it was at the bottom of the flyer. "It was a good guess. I mean, where else would you have put it? Besides, that's what I'm here to do. I'm going to fire you for taking advantage of the company you work for."

"Okay. You can do that. But I'm going to ask Officer Bonner to come to the office with me so that I can get my things." Ace said that wasn't going to happen. Herb stood up, and Ace stretched his body as much as he could to seem bigger than he was. "Officer Bonner, he's firing me for unjust causes, and I'd like to make sure that I'm covered in the event that he tries to blame something that is going on illegally on me. This is my attorney, Randy Wilson, and he's going to go with us as well."

"Since you're accusing my client of cheating the good people of this town by making a profit off of donated items,

I'd like to see what you have against him in this. Also, Mr. Prince will have a chance to show what he's got on this." Randy winked at him and said he was ready.

After telling the waitress that they'd be back, they headed to his office.

Kylan was surprised to see Harper there. With her was Meggie, and a man that he didn't know. Harper had her camera on the desk. She wasn't touching it, but he'd bet anything that she was capturing everything that was going on. Kylan hoped so—he might have bitten off more than he could chew up and spit out today.

Chapter 10

Bryant watched Ace talk to his little brother. He wanted to go there now, tear him a new ass, and then beat the living shit out of him. Kylan could well take care of himself, but things were a little out of hand for him, and he hoped that Harper was right about this man. He didn't know his ass from a hole in a brown paper bag.

Was that the way the saying went? Bryant wasn't sure, but he liked it. Looking through the camera lens that was recording everything, including sound, he hoped this was going to work. It would certainly help Kylan get his own business running so that they could have their own advertising firm.

Bryant had been surprised by the overwhelming amount of businesses that Harper, and now him, were part to full owners in. Not only was there the cable companies that they now owned all of, but there were a few video rental places, second hand clothing, and baby furniture stores. As of yesterday, Randy told them that they had controlling interest in two other businesses that he didn't know what they did. He hoped it was something legal. This shit of people taking advantage of his family was for the birds.

"Mr. Prince?" He told the man to call him Bryant. "Do I need to know what is going on in there? Because to be honest with you, I'm clueless."

"See that computer over there, Mr. Sheppard? If you turn on the screen and then push in the code that is written down there, you'll be able to see everything on the computer that they're looking at. Right now, there are just a lot of he said, he said things being thrown around." Mr. Sheppard smiled when he was able to see what was going on. "Has Mr. Miller worked for you for very long, sir?"

Mr. Conway Sheppard was the owner of C.P. Sheppard Advertising, which had been in business for the last seventy-seven years. This particular Sheppard had no children to take over the business, and he'd told Harper and Bryant that he was going to sell out and move to Florida with his boyfriend and lover. Today he was going to find out why his company was having so many issues in trying to meet deadlines, and why nothing coming out of the place was up to par, as it had been before the last few years.

"This man here, Ace? He's trying to say that young Prince there is doing some underhanded things with flyers. With donations of some sort." Bryant explained to him what he knew. "I see. So, these not for profits are lining the pockets of Ace and someone that is in charge of the donations, correct?"

"You don't think my brother is doing what he's accusing him of?" Mr. Sheppard laughed. "You're a good man, smart too, so I'm thinking you have a very good reason for not laying the blame at Kylan's feet."

"Well, I've met your wife and those brothers of yours over the last couple of hours. And your momma, she's a hoot, but no one that I'd want to tangle with. Your father seems to be level headed and a very honest man. I would think that if Kylan there was doing some shady business, you'd all have him skinned alive in no time at all." Bryant laughed with him. "Bryant, may I ask you a personal question? You don't have to answer me, but I'd like to know. Is it true that you're all black tigers?"

"Yes." There wasn't any reason to lie to the man. He had come here with only their word that something was going on. And for reasons that he couldn't explain, Mr. Sheppard had trusted him—a great deal, as a matter of fact. "We're not shifters like others, Mr. Sheppard. We were tigers before we were made into men. A great and wonderful person wanted us, as the first black tigers, to spread our magic to other tigers so that there would be an abundance of tigers for the enjoyment of others." He nodded, then looked at him with a sharp look. "Yes, we're very old—thousands of years old."

"I see." Sheppard looked at the monitor again and didn't say anything for several moments. Kylan was standing behind the attorney for Mr. Sheppard, Mr. Day, walking him through the work that had been his to do, but they were not bringing up much. "He's a clever man, that brother of yours. I'm assuming that he has his work and other things on a thumb drive, correct?"

"Yes. He loves the organization of straight lines and getting things to balance out, so to speak. It's what he does. His spreadsheet that he uses for projects is detailed and up to date. Kylan has been doing that since his first day on the job six years ago. He's going to nail Ace to the wall when

145

they ask him for his thumb drive." Sheppard laughed again, and it made Bryant think of the Santa that was always in the mall around the holidays. "Mr. Sheppard, are you sure you want to sell out? I mean, after you get rid of Ace, which I'm assuming you will, it could be a very profitable company."

"I'm very sure. And to be honest with you, Bryant, I'm tired. Watching your brother work earlier when he was oblivious to anyone watching him, I could see a man that my father would have wanted working this place. A man very proud of what he does, as well as a good man when it comes to just being a friendly person to the other staff members." Bryant told him that his parents had raised them all to be such men. "Yes, I can see that as well. But you boys—men, I guess—stuck with it. You didn't get out on your own and do things the wrong way. Most people nowadays, as far as I'm concerned, have no grit when it comes to making a name for themselves. Nor do they have what it takes to be someone you know upon first meeting that you can trust with your life. I like that about all of you gentlemen."

"Thank you. I'll tell my mom when I see her tonight for dinner." He said that she'd invited him as well. "Good, then you can tell her. I'm sure that it'll mean more from you than it would from me."

Bryant watched as Mr. Day plugged in the drive that Kylan had given him, and captured the fit that Ace was having about stealing property, and that Kylan had to have taken the thumb drive from Ace's desk. Mr. Day looked at Ace.

"Are you claiming that this thumb drive is yours, Mr. Miller? I'm sorry about that then." He got up from the desk and pointed to Ace. "We've not put in the password as yet, Mr. Miller. Come here and do that. We'll wait for you to bring

146

up the work that you're claiming as your own. I'm sure if you know the way to get into the program, you'll also be able to tell us how the spreadsheet works, correct?"

"He's probably changed it by now. I wouldn't put anything past him." The police had arrived now and were standing by the doors, keeping everyone in the place. It didn't look to him like anyone was trying to leave—they wanted to see what was going on as well. "Get back to work, the lot of you. I swear, what is it I'm paying you for anyway?"

"You still owe me for overtime from two months ago."

Another employee stood up and smiled. "I've yet to receive my promised bonus for working for you on a Saturday instead of spending time with my kids."

More and more employees stood up, yet didn't leave. This was a good deal worse than any of them had thought it was.

Mr. Day looked at Kylan. "Does he owe you for overtime as well, young man?" Kylan looked at Ace and nodded. "Anything else that he owes you for? Come come now, I'm sure that there is a great deal more."

"He cashed out my bonus check two weeks ago. It was for art that I did for dog food. He claimed that he'd done all the work and I only was there in spirit. I wasn't entitled to anything, as I hadn't done what he'd told me. I saw what he turned in. It wasn't my work. I'd never turn in anything remotely as bad as that." Mr. Day asked if he had a copy of what he'd done. "Yes, sir. It's all on the drive. My drive."

Twenty minutes after Kylan put in his password, it was obvious to everyone there that Ace had no idea what he was doing. Kylan told Mr. Day that the work was locked by password and Ace couldn't change anything. But he could bring it up, if he knew how. Then Kylan was given access to pull up the files.

It was all there, just as he said it was. His art work, the notes on what was to be done with it. Also, thankfully, the paperwork that Ace had handwritten for Kylan to do for the nonprofits. There were several of them too.

"Well, this explains a great deal. I checked with the local pantry, as well as the church that was running the coat drive, and they have a great deal of everything left over, and were thinking seriously of abandoning the drives in favor of fixing up their church. With the prices that the poor citizens were being charged for things that no one paid for, it's small wonder that they were able to have any of it go to the needy." Mr. Day looked at Ace and smiled. "What do you have to say for yourself, Mr. Miller? This, what you've done in the name of this business and against this young man, is against the law."

"He's guilty. Why are you looking to me for this? All he has is a bunch of notes that he made on his own that claims that I told him to do this." Kylan pulled up the copies of papers that Ace had handed over to Kylan. There was no mistaking the handwriting. "Why the fuck are you saving every little piece of shit that you get? Don't you have any idea how much trouble we're going to be in? Christ, I'm going to have to fire you, I'm afraid. You've been undermining my work all along, it seems."

"I'll be the one doing the firing." Bryant hadn't even seen Mr. Sheppard leave the area they were in. Ace was now falling all over himself, trying to backpedal on several things as well as pointing the finger at Kylan. Ignoring him, Sheppard looked at Kylan. "You, young man—I've been keeping an eye on you. I think you'd be the one that should run this company.

How about we have a couple of beers and talk it over?"

The two of them left. Kylan would do a good job running this place, but Bryant hoped that he'd turn him down. Mr. Day stood there while Ace was arrested and taken away before he left to go with Sheppard and Kylan.

Bryant looked at Harper when they were alone, the police having sent everyone home until further notice, and smiled at her.

"Do you think that it ever occurred to Ace that he was going to get caught today?" Bryant laughed and said that he didn't think Ace had figured out that he had been caught yet. "Yes, you're probably right about that. He is sort of stupid. And that name? What the hell sort of person names their kid Ace? Like he's something sharp. Christ, he'd be lucky if he could get himself out of his home without written instructions, I'm betting."

"I love you, Harper." She smiled up at him and his heart actually skipped a beat. "I have been working on something for you. Well, me too, but mostly with you in mind."

"What?" He said that it had taken some doing—he'd not ever used money like he had with this surprise. "I don't know if you know this about me or not, but I really hate surprises. They usually mean that I'm getting something that I don't want."

"I'm going to put you on a plane and take you to a very secluded place, and take you every way that I can think of. Some of them I'll make up. We're going to lay on the beach and drink pretty glasses of whatever we want, and make love there too." She asked if the person serving them drinks was going to be watching them. "No, we'll be all alone there. I'm to understand from your brother that you own this particular island. And the only way to get there is to fly in then take a boat over. Right?"

"Yes." She was aroused, and he could smell her. "All that is there is a house. Running water was put in when the house was built. There isn't any furniture in the place, however."

"There is now, love. A big bed that I plan on using every day we're there. Also, a large shower that I plan to take you against the wall in. The fridge, also recently added with the freezer, is full. We have everything we need to make sure that we don't starve. No Internet, no phones, and certainly no one to come and find us when they have an issue." She said that she liked helping out. "I do as well. But I like having you naked and beneath me even more, my dear. But before we go, I've got everything set up so that you become my wife officially. We're going to the courthouse with my parents, then we're going to leave. No one, and I mean no one, is going to know where we are."

~*~

The wedding was beautiful. Not only were there so many flowers around the courtroom, Harper thought that someone had good taste in colors by the way the brothers were in tuxedos that matched their mother's dress, as well as the flowers. Buck had given her away. Meggie was her bridesmaid, and her brothers were there as well. It was more than she could have imagined, and so much more than she could have hoped for. It was perfect.

Harper looked down at her ring as the plane taxied to the end of the runway and took to the skies. It was made from one of the gems that had been in the bottom of the safe. The black diamond, beautifully cut and set in a tiffany setting, looked amazing on the wide gold band. No other stones were on the

150

wedding ring, which made the set look just as custom made as she wanted. This set, she knew, had come from Bryant's heart.

"I had help. You know that, don't you?" She looked at Bryant and knew that forever he would own her heart. "Aurora helped me out by forming the stone for me. It was just a hunk of diamond when I gave it to her. And when she gave it back not two minutes later, it was set on the band just like it is now. She told me that she saw it in my mind, and couldn't have tweaked it at all to make it look more perfect. Just like my bride, perfect in every way."

Harper was so emotional that she could only lay her head on his shoulder. Bryant held her for the rest of the trip, and she found herself dozing off and on. When awake, she was thinking about everything that had changed in her life over course of a few weeks. There wasn't any way that she could have planned for something like this, and she was glad to have a partner to share it with. Bryant made everything seem seamless to her. Anything that she wanted to do, he was right behind her the entire time. It was wonderful having someone so supportive, as well as loving.

The island they were going to was off the coast of California. It was hilly, lush, and full of the most beautiful trees that she'd ever seen. There were also animals galore that she had taken pictures of that she had planned on showing in the house that she had plans of building. But this, Harper thought, was so much better — to share her home with the man that she so dearly loved.

Bryant had also saved her. Her life hadn't been as perfect as she'd told herself it was. Harper had been happy, yes, she knew that. But that was all she'd been. She'd just been happy. Not in love. Not finding things every day that would remind her that she was a survivor. There were times when she would, before Bryant, fall back into a fear so deeply that she'd have to curl into a corner for days on end and wait. Harper never knew what it was she'd been waiting for until she'd met Bryant. All along he'd been her rock, someone that she could forever depend on. Her screams in the middle of the night, the sweats that she'd break out in when she heard a mother scold a child — those things were slowly fading from her life, and she'd never been so happy as she was at this very moment.

"I love you, Bryant." He kissed her and told her that he loved her as well. Then he told her to behave. "I only said that I love you."

"I can smell you. You're so aroused right now that I could and would love to strip your pants off and take you right here on my lap. Then while you were screaming out your release, I'd take us both to the floor and fuck you hard enough that you'd be unable to walk off this plane when they tell us that we're banned from ever flying again. Now, if you'd be so kind as to sit still and stop making me insane, I'd very much appreciate it."

After that she sat as still as she could. But once, when she'd had to wiggle around to get a book she'd been sitting on, he growled deeply and she felt herself getting wetter. Harper wondered if he realized that this was just as hard on her as it was him.

The jacket that she'd had on was pulled around them both, and Bryant took her hand and put it on his cock. Christ, he was thick and hard. Rubbing him, he tried to stop her, but she wanted him to suffer. Perhaps not as much as she was currently, but she wanted him to know that her needs were just as deep rooted as his were.

When he suddenly stood up, she swallowed twice when she saw that his cock was right there in front of her, wanting to just lean in and lay her cheek on what she was sure was a painful erection. Bryant jerked her up from the seat, breaking not just the seat belt that she'd forgotten to take off, but the arm of the chair too.

Giggling as he took her to the back of the plane, she felt herself getting wet enough to soak her panties as well as the skirt she had on. As soon as the door opened to the bathroom, she was shoved in ahead of him and stripped naked of everything she had on. Sitting on the sink seemed a little precarious, but she was too needy to care if they broke everything in this plane to have him inside of her.

There was no foreplay, not now. She'd been teasing him, and being as wet as she was, his hard cock filled her easily. Holding onto his back, she dug her nails deeply into his flesh to hold on. Bryant was taking her hard enough to rock the big plane.

Bryant kissed her throat, her breasts, even her shoulder. She could see his ass, tight with strong muscles, as he took her. The mirror across from them looked as if it had been put right there for her pleasure. It was the most erotic thing she'd ever seen.

"Come. Scream for me." The bite, gentle on her throat, brought her over the edge. Harper forgot where they were — or more than likely, her mind told her, she just didn't give a shit. Screaming out her release, inhaling deeply when the second climax took her, her body bowed toward Bryant, her entire being seeming to just totter on the edge of coming again. Then he bit her in the throat.

The pain was extraordinary, but brief. Coming like she was, soaring to the sky, shattering like many fireworks would on the Fourth, she came again and again. Harper needed more. Even though her body was weak with the way she'd come, the amount of times she had, Harper knew that there was more, just one more thing she need to make herself complete again.

"Come in me, Bryant. Now. I need for you to mark me as your mate. Give me your all."

He pounded her harder. The view was almost blurred, Bryant was so fast in his movements. But when he stiffened inside of her, his body poised as hers had been, she braced herself for the best release known to man.

She'd not been prepared. Nothing could have prepared her for his coming inside of her. Harper realized this a second later as her body seemed to split apart. The soar upward was breathless, the fall devasting to her body. Not in a bad way, but in the realization that it was over, perhaps. Then he came a second time.

Harper wasn't a virgin—she'd had sex after leaving home a great deal, she thought, perhaps, to prove something. Whatever it had been, the need had faded quickly and she'd been more selective of her partners. After today, she'd never be able to look at any male again and not turn her nose up at them, knowing that they'd never be able to make her feel this way.

Bryant was speaking to her. Whatever he had said, it was lost on her. Laying her head on his sweaty shoulder, Harper realized two things almost at once. They were on a plane, a plane full of other people, and she'd announced to all of them, several times, that she was coming. Looking up at Bryant, she wanted to smack the smile right off his face.

"They didn't hear us." She asked him how that was possible. "I've been around for a great long time, Harper. There are all sorts of things that I can do. You too, should you like for me to teach you. In this, I simply made the room that we're in silent. No one could hear us, and we couldn't hear them. I've never thought it was very useful until right now."

"You, my dear husband, are a mad man." The grin was cocky and sexy. "Don't think you'll be able to get away with this sort of thing again. What if your magic hadn't worked this time?"

"I never thought of that. Perhaps it didn't." Bryant wrapped his hands around her waist and helped her off the sink. "You go out first, and I'll stay here in case they did."

She did smack him then. But there was the problem of clothing. She thought about a towel, but since they were on a plane, there didn't seem to be anything but paper towels. When she looked at Bryant, he was not only dressed, but he was wearing what looked like the clothing he'd had on when they came in here.

"How the hell did you do that?" He told her it was magic. "Sure it is. How come you ripped my clothing to shreds but managed to save your own? That's not fair. Or was it your plan that I go out there naked? Men might notice."

He growled. Having no idea why what was so sexy, she folded her arms over her breasts and felt the clothing. Looking down at herself, she looked at Bryant. The brush he was using was the same one that he'd used in the hotel before they'd gotten married. Harper knew that it had been packed.

Bryant looked at her when she said his name. "Honey, it really is magic. See, while you were thinking about me—

and I thank you so much for that...." He wiggled his brows and she smacked him again. "I love you. But while thinking about clothing, you dressed yourself. It's a wonderful piece of magic that I figured out once when I had to shift to get out of nasty situations. No, you don't want to know. But suffice it to say, I'm not a rug in someone's house. Anyway, once you let yourself relax a little about the magic that we both have, I think you'll find it to be very nice and extremely helpful. We both could have done this after we made love the first time, but you were dealing with too much at the time. I thought that having real clothing to slip on would make you feel better."

"I want to be a tiger." She wasn't sure where that thought had come from, but Harper realized that was just what she wanted to do. "I want to be like you. A black tiger. Can you do that?"

He looked so profoundly hurt that she hurt herself. He didn't want her to be a tiger. Bryant would rather be one himself and leave her at home—

"Slow down. You're thinking so hard that I can feel it. But I do want you to be a tiger. I just can't change you. None of us can change anyone into what we are, especially our mates. I don't know why, but Aurora told us that later in our lives." Harper asked him what had happened. "Pops this time, he was with a friend of his and he was dying. The man, he begged to be changed to save his life. Aurora came to his aid, but told us then that it wasn't possible for us to do that. And I think she was more sorry than we were about it. But for you, I hurt deep in my heart that I can't let you feel the way I do when I'm a tiger."

He held her then, holding her to his chest, and Harper cried. It hadn't meant that much before, but now that she knew that she couldn't, it hurt. Harper decided right then and there that she was going to talk to Aurora. She'd created them, and by golly, she could fix this for her and the rest of the mates coming to the family.

They sat back in their seats, and just as he had told her, no one was the wiser as to what they'd done. Getting their dinner served to them, they shared their food and laughed, a great deal. Harper knew that she'd never forget her first time on a plane. They were officially members of the Mile or so High Club. And it had been better than anything that she could have imagined.

Chapter 11

Bryant was making it his job to make sure that Harper had a good honeymoon. As soon as the plane landed, they had a nice dinner and enjoyed the music that was playing while they ate. The maître d' knew that it was their honeymoon trip, and he had a bottle of champagne chilled for them, as well as a pretty little cake with a bride and groom on the top.

After that, Bryant took her to the opera. His family had never had the money for such things. Once, when he'd been in Paris for a walkaround, he had been able to see a street version of one of the more elaborate plays that had been new to the town, and had enjoyed himself more than he thought he might. Since then, he'd been eager to see another, but sadly, the funds were never there.

Meggie had helped him find Harper a dress to wear tonight. It was black and shimmery on her. He wanted to find a dark corner and take her as he had on the plane, but this was special for her. He could see it in every move of her body. Harper told him at the intermission that she'd never been to

159

a play before, much less a musical, and she was extremely pleased with what they were seeing.

Traveling to the hotel later, he held her while she rested on his shoulder. It had been easy making this a memory for her, a good memory, once he realized what money could buy. Bryant knew that he'd never do something like this again—not all the time at least. Money, he knew, didn't grow on trees, so he knew the value in saving. But this was special. They were man and wife, and he needed her to be happy.

"I'm exhausted. Are we taking the boat out to the island tonight?" Harper yawned hugely and he laughed, telling her that they were staying in a hotel for the night. "Good. I don't know if you know how to navigate a boat, but I'm not rested enough to try and make it work for us. I'd probably end up with us in China or something."

Before Bryant could tell her that he'd been a pirate at one time and knew well how to sail, she was sound asleep. Once they were at the hotel, he had to carry her into the huge place and to the elevator. He couldn't even get her to wake enough to have her enjoy the outside elevator that showed all of the city.

Laughing to himself, he stripped her down to her panties and then covered her up with the blankets. After making sure that she was safe and not going to roll out of bed, he sat down at the computer that he'd sent ahead for them and downloaded all the pictures he'd taken with his phone. Sending them to his parents and family, Bryant wrote a little note about each picture before going to bed. It was going to be a long and wonderful next few days, and he hoped that things were set up the way he wanted them to be.

It was close to dawn when he finished up. Deciding that

he wasn't going to bed — it was much too late for that, as they were scheduled to leave the mainland at nine — he watched the sun coming up and ordered breakfast. When Harper joined him in the dining area, he had everything all ready for her to eat. And another bottle of champagne.

"I think I'll forego the bubbly this morning. My head is not well." He got up and stood behind her, massaging her temples. "Bryant, you're spoiling me too much. Whatever will I do when I have to go back to the real world?"

"We can come out here whenever you want to get away. Before I forget to tell you, Mom sent some pictures to the new email account we have together. They're of the wedding. They're really good." She wanted to see them right now, and he got them while she finished eating. "I don't know why she sent them all — there must be a couple of hundred of them. She said that she'd make us prints of whatever ones we wanted. I hope you don't mind, but I told her that we'd decide when we got home."

"When are we going home?" He felt his heart hurt when she said that. "I don't want to leave, if that's what you're thinking. I just want to know that at some point, sadly, we're going to have to go back to the real world."

"Never, if you'd like." She said that was wonderful in theory, but not very practical. "I know, but a man can hope. We should be at the dock in a couple of hours. Want to do some shopping? It's my understanding that there is a nice street fair every day. I thought that if they had some fruits and vegetables, we could get some for our stay."

The morning was wonderful, he thought. They had had to make two trips to the dock to drop off things that they'd purchased. The stalls had everything from food stuffs to flowers—even jewelry and animals. By the time they had made other arrangements to go out to the island at noon, they were starving and excited with what they'd gotten done.

"I've only been out here once—just before I made the purchase." Harper was sitting in the back of the boat, her hair tangling around in the fast moving wind. "When I had to take a photo shoot out here, the man that brought me out, he said that the island was for sale. I thought he was joking, but it turned out that he wasn't."

"How long did you stay here?" She told him she'd only supposed to have been there for a week at the most, but had ended up staying a month. "I've never been, of course, but from the pictures that I've seen of it, it's very lovely."

"It is. It's only about a mile wide and two long. Just a long strip in the water that was made by volcanic spillage thousands of years ago." She grinned at him. "Did you notice it forming from the beginning?"

The island was everything that he could have hoped for. There were all kinds of fruits, very little of it that he could name. But coconuts were plentiful, as well as birds. He was glad now that she'd decided to bring her cameras along. He could just imagine the photos from this trip hanging in their home.

Dinner for them was steaks on the grill. They decided to eat out on the deck that was close enough to the water's edge that they could step out into the water should they want. Bryant had made sure that the house was just as he'd wanted, and after showing Harper around, they went for a swim.

Being idle was something he'd never done before. Lying on the beach with Harper while she dozed was something he thought that he might get used to. As soon as they were home, he knew that he'd have to find himself something to occupy his mind. Harper had already decided that she was going to travel less and take pictures closer to home. Bryant wasn't sure how long she could enjoy that, but he did like having her home every night.

I have a question for you. If this is a bad time, then tell me right now and I'll get back with you later. Bryant grinned, thinking that being able to talk to his family this way would certainly save on overseas charges on making a physical call. He asked Marcus what he needed. *This book that we're putting together. Do you think Harper would mind if I put both our names on the cover?*

I think she'd be pissed at you if you didn't put your name on the cover. Why do you ask? He said that he was working on the cover right now. Also, the pictures had been sent to the printer to make a mockup of the book. *That's wonderful, Marcus. You must have put a great deal of time in on this for you to be that far along.*

The most difficult part was finding only sixty pictures to put in the book. I thought about more, I really did, but Christ, what if this project fails? Bryant said that he didn't think it would. *Yes, well, you know me and what I do. I'm not very good at thinking anything will be good enough.*

I do. That's why I think that it'll be a great success. Where is the first book of pictures from? Isn't that the way you two decided to do this? One book per grouping of pictures? He told him that it was Yellowstone Park. *Great. I can see this being something that will never end. I've seen her dark room, Marcus. Even with the prints that she's made, there are about ten times that many more that she didn't print up.*

I know. When I started this project, she gave me this thick

163

binder. It was marked just like the books we're doing — places and the dates she took them. At the end of each book there are numbers corresponding to the catalog that she has them stored in at her place. Christ, for just this area alone, there are over six thousand pictures — with different dates, of course. Harp told me that she went every season to get the same pictures to show the difference in the landscape. Bryant, I don't know if you realize this or not, but she's fucking good at what she does. If you can talk her out of quitting, the world will be forever grateful to you. Bryant watched her sleep as Marcus talked more. *Also, you should know that the advertising for hiring people to work at the cable company is generating a great deal of interest. I think at last count there were over seventy-five applicants for each shift. I think having an attorney go over them first was a good idea.*

As much as I'd like to take credit for it, Harper told me that is the only way that Randy hires anyone for them. Staff included. Marcus asked what their plans were for Mark's home. *Sell it. You want it, then it's yours. It's a little out from Mom and Pop's, but you could do worse by getting it. One thing about Mark, he had expensive tastes and kept things up to par when it came to his house.*

I do want it. And the furniture, if that comes with it. I can see myself living there. Mom and I went over there the other day to look to make sure that the locks had been changed, and we took a look around. Bryant asked him if it was as modern as he thought it would be. *No, believe it or not, it's done up in woods and beautiful slate. The kitchen is a dream. The counters are concrete but not cold looking, as you might think. And the staff, they asked if they could stay should the new owners decide to sell. I told him that I'd ask you about it, so I'm asking. Not for the staff, which Randy is looking into now, but the house.*

I'll talk to Harper when she wakes up. We've been taking it easy all afternoon and into the evening. Marcus, you will have to come out here sometime. It's the most beautiful place I've ever seen. Tonight when we were swimming, we saw whales and dolphins playing in the water. Tomorrow, I'm going to try my hand at fishing. Marcus told him he was happy for the two of them. *I have never been this happy before. I'm serious. It's so calming to have a person in your life that doesn't annoy the shit out of you every time they open their mouth.*

I should hope not. Harper woke and turned to look at him. *Well, I have to get going. Talk to Harp for me and let me know. I don't want you guys to give it to me. I want it to be mine without thinking that I had to have my big brother and his wife feel sorry for me.*

Never that, Marcus, I promise. I'll let her know about the cover too.

After closing the connection, he asked Harper if she was ready for bed. "I guess we could just sleep out here all night, but I don't know what sort of creatures we'd have to fight for the beach."

"Look. But don't freak out."

He turned slowly in his chair and watched as a pair of turtles came out of the water. They were slow moving, but neither he nor Harper moved. Instead, they watched them move along the sand to the tree line and disappear. The buzzing sound from Harper was all the noise they'd made as she took picture after picture of them and the sun setting.

"I don't see turtles that often outside of the water. I love them and the way that they move. Not lazily, but with purpose. How about tomorrow we head to the center of the island and have a look around at what we can find?"

"All right. Maybe we can pack up some sandwiches and

make a day of it. Then come back here and let me ravage your body." She grinned at him and he smiled. "Have I exhausted you, my love?"

"Let's see. Since we left the airport, you've taken me in the bathroom at the airport, the restaurant where we had dinner. In one of the stalls that was empty when we were out today. Besides, I don't know if you remember this or not, but I'm only human. I can't go as much as you can." She got up and sat on his lap, her back to his chest. "I love you, Bryant. I hope that you never forget that."

"I won't. This is a promise that you can take to the grave." The two of them sat there until it was dark; the only thing that was light was the stars that shone down on them. "You never get this sort of beauty at home. Too many city lights. This place is just perfect for the two of us."

"I agree."

After making their way upstairs to their room, she laid down on the bed, naked, and he joined her in the same fashion. Tomorrow was going to be another day of fun, with just the two of them. Bryant asked her about the house and the cover, and she agreed with both. Marcus would have a home, and his name on the cover of a picture book like none other. Bryant went to sleep with a huge smile on his face.

~*~

The child was not happy. Harper had agreed to take the picture of the little girl the day after they returned from their honeymoon. Stretching her neck, Harper thought of all the things she'd rather be doing, like having her arm tatted again. Then in walked Sara.

Harper had come to love her mother-in-law. She was funny, stern, and sometimes stronger than all the men put

166

together. Not in a physical way, but just strong. And when she spoke to the mother of Clara, the little girl, Harper figured out that she too was a tiger, but an orange one.

They knew each other. The child, then, would know that tigers weren't going to hurt her. At least she hoped so. Leaning down to Clara's level, she took a tissue from the nearly empty box and wiped away the tears as she spoke. If this didn't work, Harper thought, then she was going to go back into the wild. It was easier to take a photo of a fighting hippo than it was for her to take any of little kids.

"Clara, would you like to have your picture taken so that the big tiger could sit with you?" She didn't even look at either woman when the little girl brightened up. "But tigers like Sara don't come out for crying little girls. She can only be a tiger when she's not afraid someone is going to shed tears. It makes her heart hurt. Doesn't it, Sara?"

"It certainly does. If you just sit there and let Harper take your pictures, I'll sit with you as my great black tiger, and she'll take one of you and I so that you can put it up for yourself. All right?" Clara nodded and sat up straighter. Her little bow was askew, so Sara fixed that as well. "When my tiger is with you, you're not going to be frightened, are you?"

"Heck no. I love my daddy's tiger. He's so soft and warm." Harper laughed with the rest of them. "I'm ready now, Ms. Harper. I'll be good now."

The photo shoot went so well that Harper found herself excited to want to go to the dark room now and process them. After she'd taken all that she could, having the child put on the other two outfits that the mother had brought, Sara went to the back room and came out as her cat.

Sara's cat, like Buck's, wasn't as dark as the others. The

graying around the mouth—muzzle, she guessed it was
called—was a beautiful blend of the dark fur and the graying.
After taking several pictures of Sara with the little girl, Harper
stood back and let the mother interact with the two of them.
Snapping several more pictures, Harper was sad to see them
go.

After Clara and her mom left, Sara shifted back to herself.
Even as a human, Sara was beautiful. It took her breath away
that someone so small and delicate looking had not only given
birth to six sons at once, but she was a big cat too.

"You did well. A lot better than I thought you would
when I got here." Harper told her what she'd thought earlier,
about how she'd rather be in the wild. "Yes, well, I can see
that. While they're a good family, they do push their children
a little more than I like. That little boy of theirs, Paul, he's into
every sport known around here, and I don't think there is a
single one that he likes."

"Why do they do it then?" Sara said she thought they
wanted to complain about how they were always running for
their children. "Well, that's just stupid. Why do it if you're
going to bitch about it? What does Paul like to do? And why
didn't he come to the photo shoot?"

"Oh, they'll bring him in soon enough. And the reason
that they're separate is because like all children, I suppose,
they fight a great deal. I mean, like screaming at each other
fights. But I guess they might have gotten that from their
parents. I worry about them." Harper turned when the door
opened and there stood a man and a woman. "Hello, Park.
How are you and your lovely wife getting on?"

Sara knew everyone, it seemed. No one had been surprised,
either, when she returned from the dead, so to speak. Buck

had taken Sara around, telling anyone that would listen that Sara had been living with the faerie queen. It was all right, she supposed, that it was the way for Sara to be back to life. Whatever. Really, she was just glad to see how happy Sara and Buck seemed to be all the time.

"I was wondering if I could implore you to take a few pictures for me. It's sort of out of the ordinary. Not like someone might think are normal pictures." Her mind ran right to the gutter, and she was all ready to tell them no fucking way when he continued. "You see, my family is coming to stay for the holidays, and I would like to have a family picture made with my wife."

Harper looked at the woman, who said her name was Blanche, then back at the man. She was hurt, Harper thought. Park laughed, then told her not this wife, but his first one. The children that were coming, they were hers.

"I see. Actually, I don't, but I can do whatever you wish, Mr. Peyton." Who would name their kid Parker Peyton? But it was none of her business, so Harper smiled at him. "When are your kids coming home?"

They worked out the details on the dates, then she sat down with him and asked him what sort of photos he wanted her to take. Apparently, the first missus had been gone for more than a decade. His children had taken to the winds after she passed, and this was their first time back together. They visited from time to time, of course, but not all of them at once.

"Mr. Peyton, I don't know that that's a good idea." Blanche had left with Sara to see the new display at the hardware store. Harper might be overstepping her bounds here, but she was as new to taking pictures of humans as she was being around tigers all the time. "What sort of relationship does Blanche have with your children?"

"She raised the youngest. Well, raised isn't quite right. Billy was thirteen when I married Blanche. The others, most anyway, call her Mom. Why do you think this is wrong? I don't want any of them to think I'm insane." Harper told him that she didn't think that was ever going to happen. "Thank you, my dear. But go on, tell me."

"Blanche seems like a nice person." Park said that she was amazing. "Good. How do you think she feels knowing that you're having your children, children that I'm sure she's come to love as much as you, taking pictures with your first wife? Plus, having the pictures taken by your first wife's grave marker at the cemetery is a little — well, creepy."

"I did think about that, the creepy part. But Blanche never said a word about this. She's been encouraging me all along to get— Oh my. You think she meant with her? She wanted pictures with all of us to include her too?" Harper told him that she was pretty sure she had. "Oh my goodness, Harper. What have—? She must think I'm the most horrid person ever."

"I doubt that anyone would think that of you, Park. But you really should think on this. Or simply ask her if she'd rather be a part of the photo. Better yet, just tell her that you've changed your mind, and you'd be honored to have her there. You're all family, correct?"

"Yes, we are." Park stood up, renewed by his decision, she could tell. "Thank you very much, my dear. I'm sure this will go much better. When I think of all the little hints she gave me about this affair, I want to kick myself in the bottom. To think.... Well, it matters little now. We'll do it this way for sure."

They spoke for another hour, about what sort of shots he wanted, how he wanted to have some made with his children and their families. Excitement was in the air when Blanche and Sara returned. Park kissed Blanche soundly on the mouth before swinging her around the room. They were laughing when he set her on her feet again.

"I love you, Blanche Peyton, with all my heart. If I wasn't already married to you, I'd be sure to ask you again. I think I will." Park got down on one knee and looked up at Blanche. "I love you with all that I am, my dear wife, and hope that you'll be spending the rest of your life with me and our family. When the kids get here, we're going to have all of us in one place, and the best mother is going to be right there beside me when the camera pops. Yes, ma'am, you are the best mother, friend, soul mate, that any man could have ever asked for. Will you do me the honor of forgiving me for not thinking about you when I concocted this stupid dream? From now on, love. I want you to tell me when I'm being an old fool."

They left her there with Sara. She was wiping her tears away when Harper sat down at her desk. She'd noticed that about Sara—she was very emotional at times. When she was ready to talk, she told her about Park's first wife.

"A horrid person. I know that I shouldn't gossip, but I think it might help you to know a little of the background on that couple. Park and his first wife, they never got along. All the time she was alive, she never had a kind word to say to a soul. The way she talked about Park and the kids was shameful. It was small wonder they scattered to other states when she passed away. I believe that the only reason they stayed was for their dad." Harper asked why he thought they

171

would want a picture with her. "Age and memories like that sort of fade. You want to remember the best of people after they're gone. I know that you will never think kindly of your parents, nor will the memories of them fade. But humans, that's what they do. Perhaps to give themselves the blame about how it ended. I know for a long time, Park felt that he'd failed his wife. Up until he met Blanche, he was in a dark place. But she brought him right out of it."

"Good for her. I'm glad now that I said something to him. I probably won't be able to have that much say all the time, but in this, I'm glad that I did. Thank you for helping me earlier too. If I could have, I might have shifted myself if I thought that it would work. But I'm only a lowly human." Sara looked at her oddly. "What is it?"

"Harper, you're not human. I don't know what you are now, but you're no longer human." Harper told her that she was incorrect on that. "No, love, you're more than that. Even if you weren't, you aren't lowly anything."

"Bryant told me that he couldn't change me. That it was a condition that was told to you when you were changed." Sara only nodded with a huge smile on her face. "You're starting to piss me off with that look. It might work on your kids, but not me. What the hell are you talking about?"

Sara laughed and pointed out that she was afraid of her too. Before she could tell her she was wrong, which really she wasn't, Sara sat down on one of the many displays that she'd gotten for her new digs.

"You're immortal, for one thing. I don't know if you knew that. But as I'm sure you've figured out, you can dress yourself in whatever you want. Read minds—but you'll need to practice on that." Harper said that she had gotten some magic from Bryant. "You did. A great deal of it. But if you want to work on it, I'm reasonably sure that you can shift too. Talk to Aurora. She'll be able to guide you through whatever you need."

She was going to call out to the queen as soon as she got home. If Sara was wrong, which she was sure that she wasn't, then Harper wouldn't embarrass herself by trying to figure out shifting. But she desperately wanted to be a tiger and to show her to Bryant. Closing up the shop after shoving Sara out the door, Harper headed for home. It was time to test her magic.

Chapter 12

Bryant looked at his brothers. They'd been at this all morning, interviewing people for the positions open. He thought seriously about hiring everyone that passed the background check. He said as much to his brother Harley.

"Why don't you? I mean, it's not like you don't have the positions to fill. Then we can go out into the sunshine and not have to be in this building. We should have done this elsewhere instead of in the paint smell filled rooms." The renovations were still going on, and it did smell in there. Thus the windows all being open. "By the way, don't you have to appear in court later this afternoon?"

"Yes. At three. I have to give my side of what happened the day that Mark was terminated. I have no idea why. I owned the building before he was fired, so I see no reason for judgement to be passed on to us about how we had to fire someone that worked for us." Harley said that even as long as he'd been around, he still had trouble with the judicial system. "I'm having a little trouble myself, as a matter of fact.

But Randy is going with Harper and I, so we should be well represented."

Harper and her family were at the courthouse this morning, hearing the last will of their parents for the first time in whole. That was something he didn't understand either. They knew the will and the revisions to it that the children had made. Michelle didn't receive, nor did she want, anything that might have been left to her. Other than the children, and that was slowly working its way through.

"Did I tell you that I'm going to walk the woods on the other side of where the Wilsons' house was?" Harley loved to walk. It didn't matter if he was welcome or not to walk along paths not taken, he easily made it through each area without ever getting shot at. "I'm going to take my new toy with me. I've always wanted a metal detector. And since I can afford a really nice one, that's what I got myself."

"I know that I don't really have to say this to you, but please be careful. This has been a strange summer so far, and I would like to not have to worry about anything else." Harley laughed and promised that he would. "All right. But if you need us, you know you only have to reach out to one of us and we'll be right there."

"Sure, Pops, thanks for watching over my little self." They both laughed, and when the next person sat in front of them, Harley asked if they were going to do it. When Bryant nodded, Harley grinned at the young woman in front of him. "You're hired. Just tell me which shift you want to work. If you have no preference, then that's fine too."

She told him that she'd rather have nights. Putting a two at the top of her application and having her sign it there, he told her to have a good day. Yelling next to the next person, they started moving through the line at a much better pace.

By one o'clock they were finished, for the most part. Harley left him so that he could go walking, and Bryant was only waiting on his mom and pops to come and take over the hiring process. Telling them when they arrived what they'd been doing, Pops was tickled that he'd not have to actually interview anyone. Mom liked that they were having them sign off on the shift they requested.

"What do I tell them about start date if they ask? Or training?"

Bryant told him what he had figured out. The people working for the cable company that wanted to stay with him, which was almost everyone, were going to train them. But they couldn't do anything until the building was upgraded and finished being worked on. "If they ask, tell them that we're having a dining area put in with more microwaves, fridge capacity, as well as some other perks."

"Good for you, son. Using your past experience from working here to make improvements. I remember many a night when you came home complaining about things not working out in the breakroom because of the lack of space."

"I could never understand why, when they knew there were going to be at least a hundred people working per shift, they only had room for three people to have their meal. That was costly too, having things brought in if you wanted a hot meal or something." Bryant hugged his parents before telling them where Harley had gone. "He promises to call out if he needs us."

"Bryant, I swear you worry more than I did when you boys were younger."

Nodding, he left them there as another group came into

the building. He knew his parents would be all right, but they could be talking the arm off of each person they knew. Or knew some family member. It was what he'd come to love about this area, the way everyone seemed to know everyone. That was one of the things he hated most about this area too. The way everyone knew your business.

He had walked to town this morning, and now that it was midafternoon, he was glad that he had. The little chill in the air this morning had made him think that fall was right around the corner, which he supposed in a way that it was. But right now it seemed full-on summer again, and for that he was thankful too. Spring was his favorite time of the year. The snow was fine, but spring opened up so many wonderful things that he loved to be out of doors when it happened.

The courtroom was just letting out when he got inside of the big building. Bryant saw Harper before she saw him, and all he could do was stare at her. She was dressed in a business suit—not a skirt, but a nice fitting men's type of suit. The only thing that was feminine about it was the shirt. The sleeves hung below the jacket in a ruffled cuff. The front of it was low cut, showing just enough of her cleavage to have men wondering what delights she had beneath it. Her hair was up in a pony tail that made her look ten years younger.

Harper smiled at him when she turned his way.

"You look good enough to eat, my dear." She said that he'd done that, and she needed for him to repeat it. "Why, did I miss someplace?"

"You are wonderfully thorough, my dear husband. By the way, everything is official now. Everyone has signed off on the paperwork that Randy drew up. The land and all the surrounding buildings, I guess there are a couple, are ours

178

too. Did you know that we own the rights to the waterway? It's only a creek right now, but I guess in the spring it's fast moving and floods some of the fields surrounding it." Bryant asked if there were any farms below the waterway that depended on it. "I didn't think to ask, but that should be easy enough to figure out, I would think. I never thought of that, but that could be why I got a certified letter in the mail via Randy, asking if I would remove the dam. I'll have him look into that too."

"I have to be in the courtroom in about twenty minutes, over the thing with Mark. Do you have time to sit with me?" She pouted. "Ah, I can take that as a no. More pictures?"

"Yes. When I started this, I had no thoughts of graduation pictures. They're not too bad, so long as the parents aren't in the room. They have this set thing in mind for the photos, and I can tell that the kids just want to get it over with." He laughed. "I have another shipment of props coming in today too. So if you have time after this is done, can you come over to the studio and help me sort them out? I'll make it worth your while."

Bryant laughed when she wiggled her brows at him. Before he could tell her what he had in mind for paying him for his help, the bailiff called him into the room. Kissing her on the nose, telling Harper that he loved her very much, he went into the room and sat down next to Randy. Mark was there too.

Mark didn't look the same. It took him a few seconds to realize that he looked relaxed. He had on a pair of jeans that were worn in places but clean. His shirt was a dress shirt, but not silk, as he'd been known to wear all the time. His shoes were tennis shoes that Bryant noticed had a bit of sauce on them. All in all, Mark looked like a new man. Bryant only hoped it was for the better.

The room was called to order and Mark stood up. Bryant was almost afraid to hear what things spewed from his mouth, but Mark politely asked the judge if he could say something first.

"Yes, but you well know that it will be recorded, young man. And in that, you say what you wish. But this will not be postponed. I have better things to do than to try and figure out what to do with you." Mark said that he understood. "Good. Go ahead then."

"I wasn't a good person." The judge cocked a brow at Mark as he continued. "I'm not now either, but I'm working on it. Every day, the first few days of making pizzas, I tried to find something positive that I was getting from being fired. In doing that, I figured out that Mr. Prince did me a huge favor by doing what he did."

"Are you going to drop some sort of bombshell on this now that you've gotten everyone's attention?" Mark said that he was only trying to make amends. "All right then, continue."

"I was a selfish bastard when I owned the cable company franchise. I took things that didn't belong to me. Made promises that I never had any intentions of keeping. I lied to get things to work out for me, and all I got out of that was things that I lost because of my inability to think of someone else instead of myself." Bryant watched the judge and not Mark while the younger man continued. "Bryant was the best employee that anyone ever had. He would work overtime without any fuss. The customers loved him. He was helpful not just to the people online that needed his help, but to everyone, including me. I didn't deserve such a man working for me, and for that

180

I must tell him how profoundly sorry I am."

"I'm very glad to hear that, Mr. Shaw. However, there is the matter of the money that you owe this man and a great many others. Mr. Prince is here because you owe him the greatest debt." Mark told the judge that he was willing to work on paying it all back. "I'm not sure how you intend to do that. You don't make much money now."

Bryant stood up. When he was given the chance to speak, he had to clear his throat twice before he could. It wasn't that he was moved by what Mark had said, but it was the whole of everything that he'd heard about the other man.

"Your Honor, I'm friends with Joe-Joe, the gentleman that owns the pizza place where Mr. Shaw works. He said that the day that he was fired by me, Mark came right in and asked for a job. Joe-Joe remarked on how he's never been late, works well with others, and that he's ready to show him more things he could help out with at the shop. I'm taking that as a man who has changed his life around." The judge said that he could be just playing. "He could be, Your Honor, but I don't think so. On that note, I'd like to forego any monies that Mr. Shaw owes me. Also, as a gesture of good will and paying it forward, I will clear his debt to everyone else at the cable company that he owes money to."

Mark sat down, sobbing. Walking to him, Bryant lifted his head so that he could see him, and told him that he'd do this on one condition. Mark said he'd do it, no matter what.

"You pay this forward. I want you to help someone out, or some people out. Even if it's just helping them change a tire. Giving the only change you have in your pocket to someone that might be able to use it. Pay whatever debt you can to someone that is in worse shape than you." Mark got up and hugged him. Crying the entire time, he said that he didn't deserve a person like him in his life. "You're a good man now, Mark. Work on keeping yourself that way. But if I hear one thing that you've done—"

"You won't. I can promise you that, Bryant. I'm working on being someone that I can be proud of, that isn't making it on the coattails of someone else. You've given me a great gift in this, and I swear to you on my mother's heart, I will pay this forward." Bryant believed him. "You didn't have to do this, and this just goes to show what a good person you are that I took advantage of. I'm sorry. I thank you from my heart, Bryant. Thank you for helping me."

Bryant left after paying the money to the others. It wasn't nearly as much as he'd thought it would be after taking his money off. He was worried about what Harper would say when he told her. For him, it was a great deal of money. Bryant hoped that she'd see that what he'd done was just what he'd told Mark—a way to make things better for a lot of people.

~*~

Harley was having a good time. He'd not found all that much, but it was something that he enjoyed to get away from everything. Sitting down to have a drink, he looked around the dense dark forest. That was when he noticed the stone wall.

It wasn't very big, only about three feet tall. It was in really good shape, he thought, for being as old as he thought it might be. Deciding to follow it to see where it led, he got up after putting his water away and started out on this new adventure.

Harley had heard from Harper once. She told him that she wanted him to know that the land that they owned went about seven thousand feet beyond the waterway. He didn't know why that was important to him until she finished.

Would you look for some outbuildings on either side of the water? And a dam that will be holding back the water in the spring. More than likely year round, but that would be so helpful for me to find it and take it down before we get hit with flooding again. He told her that he could do that. *Also, and this is from Bryant, he said to be careful. I would hate to see him around our children. He's going to drive them crazy with always hovering around them all the time.*

Harley was still thinking about his big brother being a father. He'd be good at it, if a little too protective. He was thinking about being an uncle, his parents being grandparents, when he found the end of the wall — and the house that it was protecting.

It was a huge house, like something that might have been built in the eighteen hundreds, with a wraparound porch that had a bay window, and a second floor one between them. The first floor porches were covered in vines now. The dark double door was fronted with a screen door, and on the other side was the same type of door, but the screen had been torn. There was even an old rocker on the porch under the front window.

Walking closer to it, he could see the big barn, which was in reasonably great shape. The curve around driveway was weedy, but still something that a person could use. Harley supposed the fact that it was so far off the beaten path was the reason that the windows were intact. Even the tri set of windows on the upper floor in the middle were still in one piece.

There wasn't any creaking sound when he walked up onto

the porch. He was excited to see what had been left behind when the house was vacated. The artist in him thought of all sorts of reasons why one would leave a house like this one. But as soon as he entered the big house, all thoughts of the people that had lived here and left it were gone.

"Good Christ almighty."

The first thing he saw was the old oak staircase, with another one on the other side of the room. They met in the middle of the second floor, where another stained glass window looked out over the back yard, he'd bet.

To his left as he walked in, the pocket doors had been closed, so he pushed them back out of his way. They moved easily, and were not warped or painted. The room held a fireplace that wasn't all that big, but the mantel would hold numerous pictures. Above the fireplace was a picture of the house when it was in all its glory. The chairs were covered in some sort of cloth, while the curtains were in bad shape and hung from the wooden rods like a beautiful dresses falling off a hanger.

Wandering into the hall again, skipping some of the rooms in favor of looking around, he saw the old grandfather clock. It was still now; he supposed it had stopped moving when there was no more heartbeat in the house. Sad, he thought, that no one depended on it to tell them when to eat or go to bed. Touching the painted glass, he wasn't surprised to find it was dusty, yet still shone in the light coming from the front windows.

The kitchen was in the back, behind what he supposed had been the parlor. It was huge too, taking up the rear of the house like it had been made to feed hundreds of people at one time. One of the staircases in there led upward to the upper floors, and while the other one went down through a flat door in the floor. The things left behind here were also a marvel for him. Things that he'd seen as he was growing up, other things that a person growing up in the time period would have wanted for his own home. Harley laughed when he saw that the dishes, all stacked up in the cabinets, were in good shape. The water pump had been painted a dark blue at one point, and he loved it.

The next room was the dining room. The table was there, but no chairs were waiting around the table to be used. The corner cabinets were filled with dishes, and what he thought had been expensive glasses that he admired for their beauty and function.

The chairs, six on both sides of the room, were hung from pegs on the walls. Across each of them was a leaf for the table. The table was about six feet by four feet now. With the foot wide leaves, he could see his growing family sitting around it. There was a fireplace in this room as well, about the same size as the one in the parlor.

Harley made his way to the second floor, mindful of the creaking stairs, but also loving the spindles that were handmade, and the beautiful woodwork on the bannister. Getting to the landing where the large stain glass window was, he could see out the back but couldn't make things out very well.

The second floor was bedrooms, and one bathroom. Six bedrooms, three on each side, shared the single toilet. The tub, copper, sat on a small heater, and he wondered at the heat of the tub when it was set to heat up.

Looking into each of the bedrooms, he realized that he'd made a mistake about them. There were only two on each side, with one at the end. This one, he thought as he entered it, was the master bedroom. A smallish room was off to the left with a single window in it, and he thought this room was the nursery, but then found a room that was filled with baby things a few minutes later. The other, he thought, was the maid's room, for both the woman of the house as well as the child.

The other bedrooms were furnished with what the master had in it—a bed, a tall boy, as well as a dresser. Each of the rooms had a closet, but they were very small, only holding a few items that might be considered nice and would fit there. The closets were empty except for the cedar floors and walls, which would have kept the moths from eating away at whatever had been put inside.

Going down the stairs on the other side, he found the living room—or he supposed it would be called the sitting room. It contained an ugly, dark blood colored couch, a desk that he loved, as well as a rocking chair and a few other pieces.

All the furniture was of good quality. If he didn't miss his bet, all of it had been handmade right there on the property. Plenty of trees stood tall and wide in the back of the house, and he thought they might even be second growth.

Iron chairs and a table occupied what had once been a decking of sorts. A fallen tree had taken out most of the wood there. Once it had been exposed to the elements, it didn't take long for it to rot away and for bugs to take advantage of it. Thankfully, none of the windows had been broken by the tree, so everything in the house had stayed safe.

After walking around in the back yard, he found an old garden, an herb garden, as well as a small orchard that held apples. There was a grape arbor too, but it had overgrown on itself, as well as the bigger trees cutting off the sunlight to it. Harley decided as he sat down on the ground to enjoy one of the fruits that he wanted to live here.

Harper, are you busy? She said she was in the dark room but otherwise not busy. *I found a house back here.*

You can have it. He laughed so that she could hear him. *I have to tell you, Harley, we're overwhelmed here with houses that pop out of nowhere. Garages filled with shit I don't know what to do with, as well as I'm to find my aunt, brothers, and sister a home to live in. What kind of house is it? And I was telling you the truth, you can have it.*

It's very old. And beautiful. With a little love and some money, I think it would be a grand house like it was at one time. She asked him if he was up to it. *Yes, I think I am. There is a great deal of furniture left behind that I can see being restored and used again. I really do want to buy this off of you and Bryant.*

Are there five bedrooms, Harley? He said that there were. *Okay, I don't know where you are in relation to the house, but on the front of it, near a stone fence, there will be a marker. All it has on it is the letter P. Can you see if that's it?*

He did what she asked and found the letter. He knew it didn't belong to her and that he was going to lose out on the deal of a lifetime. Even if she wanted millions for the house, it was something that he would have gladly paid to live here.

That does belong to us. Harley let out a long breath that he'd been holding. *The last name of the people that lived there at one time was...let me think. Parkerson. It was called the Parkerson Mansion. The paperwork said that the missus died, who had been the only one that had been nice to people, and the husband was run out of town. Something about spoiling young ladies. I'm assuming he might have raped them or something. Anyway, it was left unsold*

187

for many years while the courts looked for any children. There were two born to the Parkerson family, but neither of them lived past their twentieth year. If you're wondering how I know this, it's because when we got the specs on the land that my parents owned, that was mentioned. There is also a barn there.

I found the barn, but nothing else so far. I'm serious about buying it off of you guys. I really want this. She told him it was his. *No, I can't do that, honey. This is a find for me, and I want to pay you for it.*

What you want to do is shut up and take the fucking house. He waited for her to continue, not sure of her mood. *Please take the house. It really will take some of this off our shoulders before I pack Bryant and me up and head back to the island. We sold the house that belonged to Mark for whatever Marcus had in his pockets. Just the change, if you're persistent on buying it. But I can gift it to you, as I want to, so that neither of us are in trouble with the IRS.*

All right, I'll take it. Only if you promise me that you'll come out here and have a couple of holidays with me. Harley noticed the swarm coming toward him, and looked around for someplace to hide. Whatever they were, they were coming in fast. *I have to go. Something has come out of the woods after me.*

Harley just stopped short of swatting at the bugs when he realized that it was a group of faeries. He'd been so terrified that he had to sit down on the steps that led up to the house and breathe deeply for several minutes. The faerie that sat on his leg, Toad he said his name was, told him how sorry he was.

"It's all right. I just wasn't expecting anyone. What is it I can do for you, Toad?" He grinned, and Harley had another moment of fear. He'd never seen a faerie this close up, and was startled by his sharp teeth. "Am I in trouble?"

"No, my lord, never that. We've come to make the house beautiful again. When we heard that you had taken it, we were beside ourselves to come and fix it up. The lady of the house, Lady Parkinson, was so good to us all. Why, she'd lay out sugar cubes for us to nibble on when it was snowing, and grew the most beautiful roses and other flowers just for us. Of course, now that is all gone to sleep, but we're here to fix you right up. How do you want it to look?"

Harley didn't know what to think. But telling them that there was a picture on the front mantle that he wanted to have it look like had that little man grinning again. This time Toad seemed to be careful of not showing too many teeth.

"I'd like to bring all the furniture back too. Do you happen to know how to do that?" He nodded. "All right, you give me the name and I'll take care of it. All right?"

Instead of answering him, Toad laughed and flew away. Harley sat there for several minutes, thinking about how much work he was going to have to do before he could even live in the place. Then there was making himself a driveway to get back here. While trekking in the woods was fun in the summer months, he didn't relish doing it in the winter. Getting up, he turned to look where to start.

"Mother Mary and Joseph."

Chapter 13

Samson was standing in line at the bank. He didn't care for banking at all. He'd been around when the crash occurred, and being in banks was dangerous to your very life. Keeping an eye out for anything, he moved up one step, and the woman in front of him turned and glared.

He'd not touched her, not even to step on the heel of her shoe. But he told her he was sorry and that he'd be more careful next time. Samson did notice that she was carrying a bundle, and wondered if he'd ever be a father. Not now, of course—he had to find a mate first. His mind did slide to Bryant being a father.

"Excuse me." He looked at the woman and the few feet between them. "Could you please stop breathing down my neck?"

Her voice was loud, and Samson was embarrassed. He looked around and saw that she had caused the other patrons to turn and look at them. After his face heated up, his anger was right there on the surface. The cat within him got pissy too.

"I'm sorry, miss, but I don't think you have the right of it. I'm a few feet from you, and I've not been breathing anywhere on your person." People snickered, and Samson held tighter onto his temper. "I'm sorry that you feel that way, but I'm not bothering you."

It took his befuddled mind almost too long to realize what was happening. The woman dropped the cloth that had been in her arms, the one that he had mistaken for a baby, and held a gun right to his chest. He might be an immortal, but it would still hurt like hell to be shot in the chest at this range.

Firing it once into the ceiling, she screamed for everyone to get down. Two more people that had been in line with them, both males, pulled out weapons too, larger assault rifles. If he got out of this, he wanted to remember each and every one of them. But right now, Samson wanted to help, to tear the people robbing the bank up. But he'd be shot before he could shift.

He had to think of a plan to get everyone out of here safely. Samson gave two shits about the robbers. There were a great many ways to make money that didn't involve pointing a gun in someone's face. Samson was thinking that he had to act now before they got all jittery when the woman poked him in the chest again.

"What are you looking at, mother fucker?" He cocked a brow at the woman, who was about two feet shorter than him and weighed less than his boots, he thought. "You think you're so high and mighty, don't you? Well, I fucking hate men like you. So I think you're going to be the first to die."

"Really? I don't think so." He looked around at her two partners. They were both close enough that he could get to them as his tiger and not let them hurt anyone. The woman was in front of him, but if he leapt and shifted at the same time, he might get hurt, but she'd be dead.

"What if I told you that I was going to kill you. And your partners."

"I'd say that you're all fucked up in the mind." Samson asked her if she liked that word. "Which one? Fuck? What, are you a prude or something? Yeah, as a matter of fact, I do fucking like to fucking use it. Does it bother you?"

"No. But I will tell you that it shows that you are of lower intelligence, and that you have to resort to rudeness to make people believe that you're something that you strive so hard to be." She asked him what that might be. "A human being. I've decided that you're not. Not at all. A monster? More than likely. Especially if you follow through on killing us all. A careless bitch that doesn't care who sees the work she's done and looks right at the cameras every chance she gets — you're that all right. What else?"

"Don't you have any idea who it is you're talking to, fucker? I'm Lisa Dawn. My brothers and I have been robbing banks for five years, and nobody has even come close to catching us." The guns went off again, and he realized that he might have heard of them, but he wasn't sure. "Am I striking you with fear, mother fucker?"

"Striking me? That's not the proper way to say that, Lisa. It's 'Am I striking fear in your heart?' Not that I believe you have one. Or, 'Do I look stricken with fear?' Which, by the way, you really should be." She pointed out again that she was Lisa Dawn. "So? I'm Samson Prince. Things like I've determined you are don't scare me at all. Only in that if you were to breed, then I'd be terrified of what sort of thing you'd spawn. By the way, are you by chance sleeping with one or both of your brothers? That would be even more terrifying."

The gun butt hit him in the chin. Samson was a big man, as she'd pointed out to him, so it only cocked his head to the right. Taking advantage of the gun no longer pointing at his chest, he let his hand morph before he shifted, and swiped at Lisa Dawn's throat before leaping onto the other two.

The first one went down quickly. Samson had hit him right in the middle of his chest and heard the gun go off. The sting of something hitting him in the shoulder just pissed him off. His cat wanted to kill, knowing that if he didn't act fast, someone might get hurt. Samson didn't want it to be him, if at all possible.

The second man had started running—just what his cat wanted…to play. As he jumped over the counter at him, another shot went off and he felt this one hit him as well. Running the man down but not killing him, he held him with his paw on his chest as he looked down at the man.

He couldn't have been any more than fifteen years old, if that. Samson remembered something that his mom used to say about having just enough whiskers to have a cat lick them off. This wasn't even possible with this child. He held him there as the air around him was permeated with the smell of hot, fear filled urine.

"Samson?" He didn't move as he held the boy down. He'd been thinking of his own wounds that were making him a little weak. When he heard his name again, he growled at his pops before telling him to go away. "I can't do that, son. The police are here, and they want you to take off before they come in. Said that the newspapers caught wind of this group being in town."

They were going to kill us all. Pops said that he knew that too. He knew just who they were. *This is just a kid, Pops. He no more needed to be here than any of these people did to be shot.*

"Yes, I know that too, son. But he's got himself a long list of murders. This boy killed his mom and pop about a year ago, when they wouldn't allow him to quit school and join his sister and brother on the road. We might not ever know what they needed to do this for, but that's not our decision. You go on out the back way. Kylan is out there waiting on you. He's got you some food and water, as well as his truck. You go now, Samson. Saving these people was a good thing you did. But it isn't any reason for you to get yourself into trouble with the bad guys. And once you're healed no one will be the wiser."

Letting the kid go, but not before licking his face, he told his pops to tell the kid what he said. That he knew him now, and if he was to escape, he would be as dead as his sister. Samson went out the back way of the bank, and was surrounded by the police before his mom came to rescue him. Kylan met him and they headed to the truck, but Samson decided he needed something, a little run.

"I understand that, Samson, but you be careful. The police know you and us, but they're a little on edge. These people were wanted by the FBI, and you took them out. I hope you don't mind, but Pops is going to tell the police that they were the ones that saved them people just to keep you safe. No one in the bank will say any different."

Samson told his brother he didn't care and took off toward the woods.

The need to sweat the smell of the dead off of him was beating at him. His cat, normally so calm, wanted to go back and kill again. But they both knew that it was over for them, and that everything was fine now. Running to the little creek that ran through Bryant's property, just for a place to head, he found the dam.

It had been built with the intentions of never coming apart. What he saw there was human waste — that someone, in their own greed, had killed off the animals that now lay by the lower part of the dam, dead. Beavers and other animals depended on the running water, and he knew that the Wilsons had taken great pride in putting the sucker up. Well, it was time to take it down.

It took him nearly an hour to break away one part of it with his hands after he'd shifted. Picking up heavier stones that he used as hammers was easier for him than it would have been for a human. By the time his brothers showed up with a pair of swimming trunks for him, he was ready to call it a day. But it needed to be done, and with the extra help, they would do it sooner.

Instead of just tossing the stones, some of which were a good size, they began stacking them in a way that would curve the waterway back into its original path. With the water only a trickle most of the time, it had moved in an easier way, and that was where the flooding had come into play.

"Samson, did you hear? Harley and Marcus each have them a house. When are you getting one?" He smiled at Fisher and tossed a small fish at him. "Very funny. Want me to tell your mate when she comes how you managed to pick out your name?"

"I don't care. I'm sure that sooner or later, she'll hear about it." The cat coming toward them made them all pause. Bryant was standing closest to him, and he poked him when he didn't stop working. "I don't know that cat, do you?"

"It's Harper." Samson looked at his brother so quickly that he nearly slipped in the water. "Don't tell her I told you — she wants you guys to guess who she is. I don't know if she realizes this or not, but if she gets much closer, you'll smell her anyway."

Samson kept an eye on the younger woman. She was new to walking on four feet, and it showed. But what didn't show was her fear of being a big cat. When she laid down by the water, next to his mom, he tipped an imaginary hat at her.

I didn't think you'd know me. Samson told her what Bryant had said about smelling her. Not that Bryant had told him, but that he could smell her. *Oh, I didn't think of that. Bryant said I'm a pretty cat. Well, that's not actually what he said, but my version will embarrass both of us less.*

Samson burst out laughing. She was a pistol, Harper was. He was glad that she was part of his family now. He asked her about the to-do in town, the robbery and such. She shifted and was dressed in one smooth movement. Samson was proud of her for that.

"The robbery report is going down as the police saw the robbers enter the building, and entered before they had a chance to hurt anyone. It's going down as a little town hitting it big. Most of the townspeople are just thrilled that you were there to keep them safe. I guess they all knew about the robberies from before. I'm taking on a part-time job as photographer for the newspaper." It was a quick change of subject, but if the looks on everyone's faces were any indication, they'd caught it too. Bryant asked if she was finished with picture taking locally. "No. I've been enjoying that part of it now that I've got a reputation to uphold."

Mom snorted before speaking. "They all think that she's wacky. Like she's a batty old woman who yells and screams a lot, but takes the best pictures ever seen. Just the other day I came up on her when she was taking pictures of a bunch of those squealing teenage girls. She was screaming at them, telling them to stand still, and they all did it. I don't know if they were afraid of her or humoring her until they got finished. Then she invited them to have pizza with her. Craziest thing I've ever witnessed."

"How did the pictures turn out?" Everyone laughed when her answer to Pops was just a smile. "There's my girl. You keep them kids in line and they'll behave when they're around town. I don't believe that, but one can hope."

The dam was down. The stones that were lined up on either side of the faster moving water were keeping things where they should be. As they followed the water downstream, Harley was telling them how this water ran behind his new home, and that it was deep enough to go swimming in. Also, he was going to go fishing in it. They saw his house a few minutes before it was fully in view. It was much bigger than he'd thought it would be. But the real kicker was that it looked like it had just been built.

~*~

Allie laid her head on the bar as the man spoke to her about her sister and brothers. She knew that they'd eventually be put down like the dogs that they were, and she hadn't had anything to do with them since she'd come home from work one night and found her mom and dad in bed with bullets in their chests.

It had been Howie that had done it. At twelve he was already acting like Serenity, the leader of their little band of fools. When she realized there was a pause in the conversation, she asked him to repeat himself.

"I asked if you wanted to come and claim the bodies. Your youngest brother, Howard, is still alive, but he's in the hospital for wounds he sustained when the police came into the bank." She told him no, she wasn't claiming anything to do with them. "I'm to understand that you are related to them, correct?"

"Yes. I'm the oldest of the four of us, but I still want nothing to do with them. They made their respective beds. As far as I'm concerned, they can lie in them." He sputtered around for several seconds. "I don't know how you were able to track me down, and frankly I could care less. But we broke up being anything to do with family when they killed our parents. You want them claimed? Then I suggest you find some other sucker that knows them. This chick was finished with them a long time ago."

Hanging up the phone, she felt no better about her family than she had before. Allie supposed that she could be happy they were off this planet; they should have been killed a long time ago. But it wasn't any of her business now. When she'd left the only home she'd ever known after burying her parents, she'd gotten a restraining order against her siblings and changed her phone number and address. Never again, she thought, would they come to her for anything.

Not that they did anymore. She supposed them having more money than anyone else because of the bank robberies would make her useless to them. Again, she didn't care. They were out of her life, forever now, and she was happy for it.

"You all right, Al?" She nodded at Ben, who sat at the end of the bar where she had been on the phone. "They were killed right here in Ohio. Did you know that?"

"No. I stopped reading the news and watching it a long time ago. If it's not sports, it's not on my need to watch list." He smiled and asked for another cold one. Pulling him a beer, she slid it in front of him as she picked up the burgers at the window. "You eating tonight, Ben? We have chili cheese fries if you want them."

They didn't have an extensive menu—Allie liked that about her place. They had chili on Wednesdays, and chili cheese fries on Thursdays. That was the only consistent thing. That and burgers. In fact, at the end of the night, Charlie would cook up all the left over burger meat from that day and freeze if for the chili that week. It cut down on waste, and people came from all over town to have a bowl of his chili.

"Allie, phone."

She nodded at Charlie, who had answered it when she'd gone out to take an order. If it was that cop again, she was going to tear him a new ass. Allie had worked hard to own this place, and she wasn't going to leave it here to go and bury her family. She'd done all the laying to rest of her family that she wanted in a single lifetime.

"Allison?" She knew the voice, and closed her eyes against the pain that it caused her. "Allison, it's Howie. They're arresting me."

"What the fuck did you think was going to happen, Howie, when you went off to play big boy with Serenity and Heath? That you'd kill our parents then rob a few banks, and be able to live on easy street? No, it doesn't work that way." He started crying. It no longer worked on her; she didn't even shed them for herself any longer. He asked if she'd come to get him. "No. And if there is nothing else, leave me alone,

200

Howie. I told you once before, you are no longer my brother."

"I messed up." She didn't even bother telling him that he had. Big time. "They're saying that I'm going to go to prison for the rest of my life. Something about being tried as an adult."

"Again, what did you expect to happen? You play the murderer, Howie, you have to expect to get all the points that come with it." Howie was only fifteen now, and she felt guilty for not having some sort of emotional attachment to him. Or at least a little. "I'll tell you what I told the cops — don't call me again. I don't want, nor do I need, you in my life."

Hanging up the phone, she made her way out to the bar again. Ben was eating the cheese fries, and the place was hopping again. While she had help on the weekend and Friday nights, she did the work herself through the week.

Taking the orders of a particularly loud group of young man, she carded them all and kicked one of them out for being underage. It took the threat of calling the cops before he finally left quietly. After that, it was a smooth night, and she finished up the last drink at midnight, when she closed.

After Ben and the rest of the people in the kitchen left, she sat in her office with the money laying on the desk. She wasn't worried about anyone coming in to rob her this late at night. Not only was the locked door to her office thick steel, but she also had a gun. The panic button that she'd had put in when she'd opened the place rang right to the police. One push and they'd come running — or at least they'd better.

After counting out the till and getting things set up for tomorrow, she gathered the deposit and called for a ride. She drove — her bike was in the parking lot for her to take home. But she didn't go to the bank alone. Allie wasn't stupid enough to do that. Having a family like hers, she knew she wasn't immune to getting robbed or killed.

One of the off-duty cops pulled up and she locked up the bar.

"Why aren't you married?" She asked Morgan if he was proposing. "No. I like you, but you're hard on a man. I heard about your date with Sam. Christ, he still has those bruises you gave him. Don't you cut anyone any slack, honey?"

"Sure, if they deserve it. In his telling of his side of the story, did Sam happen to tell you that he tried to spike my drink and that I caught him at it? Then the fucker tried to talk me into just letting him fuck me, his words, so that he could go tell his buddies that he'd had the ice queen." She looked at Morgan. "Do they really call me that?"

"He does. Well, he did. Not anymore." Morgan laughed. "Well, I believe your version more than I do his. He said that you were coming on to him, and he had to literally beat you off with his fist. I could see that you weren't hurt when I saw you the next day, so that made most of us think he was lying."

"He was." She watched the trees fly by as he took her to the bank. "Morgan, Serenity and the other robbers, you know that they're related to me, don't you?"

"Yes. Most of us did. We've been keeping an eye out for them for you. Did you hear about what happened?" She nodded, then told him that she had had phone calls from the police and Howie. "I thought they might find you. They've put out an all points looking for you across the state. I'm thinking, now that you said they called you, that your buddy Sam told them where you were."

"I never thought of that. Fucker." Morgan said that he'd take care of him, and she didn't ask what that meant.

People who fucked around with the police station here were reminded in a harsh way that things were their way, or get the hell out of town. "They wanted me to claim the bodies. And then Howie called to ask me if I could come and get him. Like I might stash him away in my pocket so he doesn't have to go to prison. They're trying him as an adult."

"They would. You're not going there, are you, sweetie?" She didn't answer him, because she was getting out to drop her deposit. When she got back in the car, he eyed her with his stern look. "What are you planning to do, Allison?"

"Nothing. I swear to you, nothing at all. The only reason that I would go there is if they summoned me. And since I know that that's not going to happen, I'm going to run my bar the way I want, and move on with my life as if nothing at all happened." She looked at him. "Do you think I can do that?"

"No." Morgan started the car up and drove her back to the bar. When they got there, she got out and sat on her bike. Morgan said her name. "If you happen to go, Allie, will you let me go with you? You know that an old queen vampire like me, I'd have your back better than any of those cops there might."

"I'm not going, but if I do—which, as I said, I won't—then I'll take you." She started her bike and rode it slowly to where Morgan was standing. "I don't want to go, Morgan. You know that, don't you?"

"I know, honey. But I also know that you loved that little boy like he was your own, and you mourned the loss of him when he went with that mad dog of a sister of yours like he was dead." She said that was what she'd wanted to feel. "I'll have a bag packed up to go when you're ready. Kenny said that he'd run the bar for you while you were gone. He's a good man, you know that."

"I know that. You two love each other too, and that makes him my best friend as much as you are." She revved up the motor and grinned. "I'm taking my bike with me. It's going to be a long ride to that little town."

"I'll be ready."

When he drove away, she realized that she was going to go. And she'd more than likely claim the other two bodies while there. However, she wasn't paying for any attorney. Nor was she going to plead Howie's case. Allie only wanted to be there in case he was found not guilty. Then she might have to kill him herself.

Before You Go...

HELP AN AUTHOR

write a review

THANK YOU!

Share your voice and help guide other readers to these wonderful books. Even if it's only a line or two your reviews help readers discover the author's books so they can continue creating stories that you'll love. Login to your favorite retailer and leave a review. Thank you.

AWARD WINNING, BESTSELLING AUTHOR

Kathi Barton, winner of the Pinnacle Book Achievement award as well as a best-selling author on Amazon and All Romance books, lives in Nashport, Ohio with her husband Paul. When not creating new worlds and romance, Kathi and her husband enjoy camping and going to auctions. She can also be seen at county fairs with her husband who is an artist and potter.

Her muse, a cross between Jimmy Stewart and Hugh Jackman, brings her stories to life for her readers in a way that has them coming back time and again for more. Her favorite genre is paranormal romance with a great deal of spice. You can visit Kathi online and drop her an email if you'd like. She loves hearing from her fans. aaronskiss@gmail.com.

Follow Kathi on her blog: http://kathisbartonauthor.blogspot.com/

www.ingramcontent.com/pod-product-compliance
Lightning Source LLC
Chambersburg PA
CBHW020620180626
46810CB00007B/2863